SCIENTIFIC AMERICAN EXPLORES BIG IDEAS

Artificial Intelligence

The Editors of *Scientific American*

SCIENTIFIC AMERICAN EDUCATIONAL PUBLISHING

New York

Published in 2024 by Scientific American Educational Publishing
in association with **The Rosen Publishing Group**
2544 Clinton Street, Buffalo NY 14224

Contains material from Scientific American®, a division of Springer Nature America, Inc., reprinted by permission, as well as original material from The Rosen Publishing Group®.

First Edition

Scientific American
Lisa Pallatroni: Project Editor

Rosen Publishing
Michael Hessel-Mial: Compiling Editor
Michael Moy: Senior Graphic Designer

Cataloging-in-Publication Data
Names: Scientific American, Inc.
Title: Artificial intelligence / edited by the Scientific American Editors.
Description: New York : Scientific American Educational Publishing, 2024. |
Series: Scientific American explores big ideas | Includes glossary and index.
Identifiers: ISBN 9781725349483 (pbk.) | ISBN 9781725349490
(library bound) | ISBN 9781725349506 (ebook)
Subjects: LCSH: Artificial intelligence. | Artificial intelligence–Technological innovations.
Classification: LCC Q335.4 A785 2024 | DDC 006.3–dc23

Manufactured in the United States of America
Websites listed were live at the time of publication.

Cover: PopTika/Shutterstock.com

CPSIA Compliance Information: Batch # SACS24.
For Further Information contact Rosen Publishing at 1-800-237-9932.

CONTENTS

INTRODUCTION

Folklore about conscious, self-directed machines has existed since well before the computer. Still, true artificial intelligence has remained elusive. Early AI researchers struggled because they thought intelligence functioned like a computer, which meant that those programs could calculate but struggled to identify patterns or adjust their behavior to new situations. A series of "AI winters" followed, where interest and funding often dwindled. The trick ended up being to make AI programs more like brains, modeled after how neurons interact with one another. The artificial neural network was born.

When artificial neural nets process vast amounts of data to generate new behaviors, that practice is known as deep learning, the current most powerful iteration of artificial intelligence. It's not yet human intelligence proper; what it can do is be programmed to simulate a wide variety of specific human tasks, often better than humans themselves. Deep learning has already been put to use in an enormous range of applications: astronomy, content moderation, drug testing, and of course games like *Jeopardy!* or Go.

As artificial intelligence takes these leaps, the first impulse is to fear a "robot takeover," like in science fiction movies. As this book shows, our primary concern should be with the error or bias of those who create or use these technologies. When AI is inappropriately used in our workplaces or criminal justice system, human biases can be made worse by machines. Leading experts on artificial intelligence call for attention to bias in further development of the technology.

The articles in this title are arranged as follows. The first section showcases some of the early history of computing and AI, to give the rest of the articles context. The second section gives an overview of deep learning, which revolutionized AI research. The third section focuses on how AI is used in various research and commercial practices. The fourth section covers AI application to games and the arts. The final section explores the ethical issues in AI, with recommendations for how best to create and use these technologies.

Section 1: Artificial Intelligence in History

The Origin of Computing

By Martin Campbell-Kelly

In the standard story, the computer's evolution has been brisk and short. It starts with the giant machines warehoused in World War II–era laboratories. Microchips shrink them onto desktops, Moore's Law predicts how powerful they will become, and Microsoft capitalizes on the software. Eventually small, inexpensive devices appear that can trade stocks and beam video around the world. That is one way to approach the history of computing—the history of solid-state electronics in the past 60 years.

But computing existed long before the transistor. Ancient astronomers developed ways to predict the motion of the heavenly bodies. The Greeks deduced the shape and size of Earth. Taxes were summed; distances mapped. Always, though, computing was a human pursuit. It was arithmetic, a skill like reading or writing that helped a person make sense of the world.

The age of computing sprang from the abandonment of this limitation. Adding machines and cash registers came first, but equally critical was the quest to organize mathematical computations using what we now call "programs." The idea of a program first arose in the 1830s, a century before what we traditionally think of as the birth of the computer. Later, the modern electronic computers that came out of World War II gave rise to the notion of the universal computer—a machine capable of any kind of information processing, even including the manipulation of its own programs. These are the computers that power our world today. Yet even as computer technology has matured to the point where it is omnipresent and seemingly limitless, researchers are attempting to use fresh insights from the mind, biological systems and quantum physics to build wholly new types of machines.

The Difference Engine

In 1790, shortly after the start of the French Revolution, the government decided that the republic required a new set of maps to establish a fair system of property taxation. He also ordered a switch from the old imperial system of measurements to the new metric system. To facilitate all the conversions, the French ordinance survey office began to compute an exhaustive collection of mathematical tables.

In the 18th century, however, computations were done by hand. A factory floor of between 60 and 80 human computers added and subtracted sums to fill in line after line of the tables for the survey's Tables du Cadastre project. It was grunt work, demanding no special skills above basic numeracy and literacy. In fact, most computers were hairdressers who had lost their jobs–aristocratic hairstyles being the sort of thing that could endanger one's neck in revolutionary France.

The project took about 10 years to complete, but by then, the war-torn republic did not have the funds necessary to publish the work. The manuscript languished in the *Académie des Sciences* for decades. Then, in 1819, a promising young British scientist named Charles Babbage would view it on a visit to Paris. Babbage was 28 at the time; three years earlier he had been elected to the Royal Society, the most prominent scientific organization in Britain. He was also very knowledgeable about the world of human computers–at various times he personally supervised the construction of astronomical and actuarial tables.

On his return to England, Babbage decided he would replicate the French project not with human computers but with machinery. England at the time was in the throes of the Industrial Revolution. Jobs that had been done by human or animal labor were falling to the efficiency of the machine. Babbage saw the power of this world of steam and brawn, of interchangeable parts and mechanization, and realized that it could replace not just muscle but the work of minds.

He proposed the construction of his Calculating Engine in 1822 and secured government funding in 1824. For the next decade he immersed himself in the world of manufacturing, seeking the best technologies with which to construct his engine.

In 1833 Babbage celebrated his annus mirabilis. That year he not only produced a functioning model of his calculating machine (which he called the Difference Engine) but also published his classic *Economy of Machinery and Manufactures*, establishing his reputation as the world's leading industrial economist. He held Saturday evening soirees at his home in Devonshire Street in London, which were attended by the front rank of society. At these gatherings the model Difference Engine was placed on display as a conversation piece.

A year later Babbage abandoned the Difference Engine for a much grander vision that he called the Analytical Engine. Whereas the Difference Engine had been limited to the single task of table making, the Analytical Engine would be capable of any mathematical calculation. Like a modern computer, it would have a processor that performed arithmetic (the "mill"), memory to hold numbers (the "store"), and the ability to alter its function via user input, in this case by punched cards. In short, it was a computer conceived in Victorian technology.

Babbage's decision to abandon the Difference Engine for the Analytical Engine was not well received, however, and the government demurred to supply him with additional funds. Undeterred, he produced thousands of pages of detailed notes and machine drawings in the hope that the government would one day fund construction. It was not until the 1970s, well into the computer age, that modern scholars studied these papers for the first time. The Analytical Engine was, as one of those scholars remarked, almost like looking at a modern computer designed on another planet.

The Dark Ages

Babbage's vision, in essence, was digital computing. Like today's devices, such machines manipulate numbers (or digits) according to a set of instructions and produce a precise numerical result.

Yet after Babbage's failure, computation entered what English mathematician L. J. Comrie called the Dark Age of digital computing–a period that lasted into World War II. During this time, computation was done primarily with so-called analog computers, machines that model a system using a mechanical analog. Suppose, for example, an astronomer would like to predict the time of an event such as a solar eclipse. To do this digitally, she would numerically solve Kepler's laws of motion. She could also create an analog computer, a model solar system made of gears and levers (or a simple electronic circuit) that would allow her to "run" time into the future.

Before World War II, the most sophisticated practical analog computing instrument was the Differential Analyzer, developed by Vannevar Bush at the Massachusetts Institute of Technology in 1929. At that time, the U.S. was investing heavily in rural electrification, and Bush was investigating electrical transmission. Such problems could be encoded in ordinary differential equations, but these were very time-consuming to solve. The Differential Analyzer allowed for an approximate solution without any numerical processing. The machine was physically quite large–it filled a good-size laboratory–and was something of a Rube Goldberg construction of gears and rotating shafts. To "program" the machine, technicians connected the various subunits of the device using screwdrivers, spanners and lead hammers. Though laborious to set up, once done the apparatus could solve in minutes equations that would take several days by hand. A dozen copies of the machine were built in the U.S. and England.

One of these copies made its way to the U.S. Army's Aberdeen Proving Ground in Maryland, the facility responsible for readying field weapons for deployment. To aim artillery at a target of known range, soldiers had to set the vertical and horizontal angles (the elevation and azimuth) of the barrel so that the fired shell would follow the desired parabolic trajectory–soaring skyward before dropping onto the target. They selected the angles out of a firing table that contained numerous entries for various target distances and geographic conditions.

Every entry in the firing table required the integration of an ordinary differential equation. An on-site team of 200 computers would take two to three days to do each calculation by hand. The Differential Analyzer, in contrast, would need only about 20 minutes.

Everything is Change

On December 7, 1941, Japanese forces attacked the U.S. Naval base at Pearl Harbor. The U.S. was at war. Mobilization meant the army needed ever more firing tables, each of which contained about 3,000 entries. Even with the Differential Analyzer, the backlog of calculations at Aberdeen was mounting.

Eighty miles up the road from Aberdeen, the Moore School of Electrical Engineering at the University of Pennsylvania had its own differential analyzer. In the spring of 1942 a 35-year-old instructor at the school named John W. Mauchly had an idea for how to speed up calculations: construct an "electronic computor" [sic] that would use vacuum tubes in place of the mechanical components. Mauchly, a bespectacled, theoretically-minded individual, probably would not have been able to build the machine on his own. But he found his complement in an energetic young researcher at the school named J. Presper ("Pres") Eckert, who had already showed sparks of engineering genius.

A year after Mauchly made his original proposal, following various accidental and bureaucratic delays, it found its way to Lieutenant Herman Goldstine, a 30-year-old Ph.D. in mathematics from the University of Chicago who was the technical liaison officer between Aberdeen and the Moore School. Within days Goldstine got the go-ahead for the project. Construction of the ENIAC–for Electronic Numerical Integrator and Computer–began on April 9, 1943. It was Eckert's 23rd birthday.

Many engineers had serious doubts about whether the ENIAC would ever be successful. Conventional wisdom held that the life of a vacuum tube was about 3,000 hours, and the ENIAC's initial design called for 5,000 tubes. At that failure rate, the machine would not function for more than a few minutes before a broken tube put it out of action. Eckert, however, understood that the tubes tended to fail under the stress of being turned on or off. He knew it was for that reason radio stations never turned off their transmission tubes. If tubes were operated significantly below their rated voltage, they would last longer still. (The total number of tubes would grow to 18,000 by the time the machine was complete.)

Eckert and his team completed the ENIAC in two and a half years. The finished machine was an engineering tour de force, a 30-ton behemoth that consumed 150 kilowatts of power. The machine could perform 5,000 additions per second and compute a trajectory in less time than a shell took to reach its real-life target. It was also a prime example of the role that serendipity often plays in invention: although the Moore School was not then a leading computing research facility, it happened to be in the right location at the right time with the right people.

Yet the ENIAC was finished in 1945, too late to help in the war effort. It was also limited in its capabilities. It could store only up to 20 numbers at a time. Programming the machine took days and required manipulating a patchwork of cables that resembled the inside of a busy telephone exchange. Moreover, the ENIAC was designed to solve ordinary differential equations. Some challenges–notably, the calculations required for the Manhattan Project–required the solution of partial differential equations.

John von Neumann was a consultant to the Manhattan Project when he learned of the ENIAC on a visit to Aberdeen in the summer of 1944. Born in 1903 into a wealthy Hungarian banking family, von Neumann was a mathematical prodigy who tore through his education. By 23 he had become the youngest ever privatdocent (the approximate equivalent of an associate professor) at the University of Berlin. In 1930 he emigrated to the U.S., where he joined Albert Einstein and Kurt Gödel as one of first faculty members of the Institute for Advanced Study in Princeton, N.J. He became a naturalized U.S. citizen in 1937.

Von Neumann quickly recognized the power of the machine's computation, and in the several months after his visit to Aberdeen, he joined in meetings with Eckert, Mauchly, Goldstine and Arthur Burks–another Moore School instructor–to hammer out the design of a successor machine, the Electronic Discrete Variable Automatic Computer, or EDVAC.

The EDVAC was a huge improvement over the ENIAC. Von Neumann introduced the ideas and nomenclature of Warren McCulloch and Walter Pitts, neuroscientists who had developed a theory of the logical operations of the brain (this is where we get the term computer "memory"). He thought of the machine as being made of five core parts: *Memory* held not just numerical data but also the instructions for operation. An arithmetic unit performed arithmetic options. An *input* "organ" enabled the transfer of programs and data into memory, and an *output* organ recorded the results of computation. Finally, a *control unit* coordinated the entire system.

This layout, or architecture, makes it possible to change the computer's program without altering the physical structure of the machine. Programs were held in memory and could be modified in a trice. Moreover, a program could manipulate its own instructions. This feature would not only enable von Neumann to solve his partial differential equations, it would confer a powerful flexibility that forms the very heart of modern computer science.

In June 1945 von Neumann wrote his classic *First Draft of a Report on the EDVAC* on behalf of the group. In spite of its unfinished status, it was rapidly circulated among the computing cognoscenti with two consequences. First, there never was a second draft. Second, von Neumann ended up with most of the credit for the invention.

Machine Evolution

The subsequent 60-year diffusion of the computer within society is a long story that has to be told in another place. Perhaps the single most remarkable development was that the computer–originally designed for mathematical calculations–turned out, with the right software, to be infinitely adaptable to different uses, from business data processing to personal computing to the construction of a global information network.

We can think of computer development as having taken place along three vectors–hardware, software and architecture. The improvements in hardware over the past 50 years are legendary. Bulky electronic tubes gave way in the late 1950s to "discrete" transistors–that is, single transistors individually soldered into place. In the mid-1960s microcircuits connected several transistors–then hundreds of transistors, then thousands of transistors–on a silicon "chip." The microprocessor, developed in the early 1970s, held a complete computer processing unit on a chip. The microprocessor gave rise to the PC and now controls devices ranging from sprinkler systems to ballistic missiles.

The challenges of software were more subtle. In 1947 and 1948 von Neumann and Goldstine produced a series of reports called *Planning and Coding of Problems for an Electronic Computing Instrument.* In these reports they set down dozens of routines for mathematical computation with the expectation that some lowly "coder" would be able to effortlessly convert them into working programs. It was not to be. The process of writing programs and getting them to work was excruciatingly difficult. The first to make this discovery was Maurice Wilkes, the University of Cambridge computer scientist who had created the first practical stored-program computer. In his *Memoirs*, Wilkes ruefully recalled the very moment in 1949 when "the realization came over me with full force that a good part of the remainder of my life was going to be spent in finding the errors in my own programs."

He and others at Cambridge developed a method of writing computer instructions in a symbolic form that made the whole job easier and less error prone. The computer would take this symbolic language and then convert it into binary. IBM introduced the programming language Fortran in 1957, which greatly simplified the writing of scientific and mathematical programs. At Dartmouth College in 1964, educator John G. Kemeny and computer scientist Thomas E. Kurtz invented Basic, a simple but mighty programming language intended to democratize computing and bring it to the entire undergraduate population. With Basic even schoolkids–the young Bill Gates among them–could begin to write their own programs.

In contrast, computer architecture–that is, the logical arrangement of subsystems that make up a computer–has barely evolved. Nearly every machine in use today shares its basic architecture with the stored program computer of 1945. The situation mirrors that of the gasoline-powered automobile–the years have seen many technical refinements and efficiency improvements in both, but the basic design is largely the same. And although it is certainly possible to design a radically better device, both have achieved what historians of technology call "closure." Investments over the decades have produced such excellent gains that no one has had a compelling reason to invest in an alternative.

Yet there are multiple possibilities for radical evolution. For example, in the 1980s interest ran high in so-called massively parallel machines, which contained thousands of computing elements operating simultaneously, designed for computationally intensive tasks such as weather forecasting and atomic weapons research. Computer scientists have also looked to the human brain for inspiration. We now know that the brain is not a general-purpose computer made from gray matter. Rather it contains specialized processing centers for different tasks, such as face recognition or speech understanding. Scientists are harnessing these ideas in "neural networks" for applications such as automobile license plate identification and iris recognition. They could be the next step in a centuries-old process: embedding the powers of the mind in the guts of a machine.

About the Author

Martin Campbell-Kelly is a professor in the department of computer science at the University of Warwick in England, where he specializes in the history of computing. He is author of Computer: A History of the Information Machine *(along with William Aspray) and of* From Airline Reservations to Sonic the Hedgehog: A History of the Software Industry. *He is editor of* The Works of Charles Babbage.

Cybernetics

By Norbert Wiener

Cybernetics is a word invented to define a new field in science. It combines under one heading the study of what in a human context is sometimes loosely described as thinking and in engineering is known as control and communication. In other words, cybernetics attempts to find the common elements in the functioning of automatic machines and of the human nervous system, and to develop a theory which will cover the entire field of control and communication in machines and in living organisms.

It is well known that between the most complex activities of the human brain and the operations of a simple adding machine there is a wide area where brain and machine overlap. In their more elaborate forms, modern computing machines are capable of memory, association, choice and many other brain functions. Indeed, the experts have gone so far in the elaboration of such machines that we can say the human brain behaves very much like the machines. The construction of more and more complex mechanisms actually is bringing us closer to an understanding of how the brain itself operates.

The word cybernetics is taken from the Greek *kybernetes*, meaning steersman. From the same Greek word, through the Latin corruption *gubernator*, came the term governor, which has been used for a long time to designate a certain type of control mechanism, and was the title of a brilliant study written by the Scottish physicist James Clerk Maxwell 80 years ago. The basic concept which both Maxwell and the investigators of cybernetics mean to describe by the choice of this term is that of a feedback mechanism, which is especially well represented by the steering engine of a ship. Its meaning is made clear by the following example.

Suppose that I pick up a pencil. To do this I have to move certain muscles. Only an expert anatomist knows what all these muscles are, and even an anatomist could hardly perform the act by a conscious exertion of the will to contract each muscle concerned in succession. Actually what we will is not to move individual muscles but to pick up the pencil. Once we have determined on this, the motion of the arm and hand proceeds in such a way that we may say that the amount by which the pencil is not yet picked up is decreased at each stage. This part of the action is not in full consciousness. To perform an action in such a manner, there must be a report to the nervous system, conscious or unconscious, of the amount by which we have failed to pick up the pencil at each instant. The report may be visual, at least in part, but it is more generally kinesthetic, or to use a term now in vogue, proprioceptive. If the proprioceptive sensations are wanting, and we do not replace them by a visual or other substitute, we are unable to perform the act of picking up the pencil, and find ourselves in a state known as ataxia. On the other hand, an excessive feedback is likely to be just as serious a handicap. In the latter case the muscles overshoot the mark and go into an uncontrollable oscillation. This condition, often associated with injury to the cerebellum, is known as purpose tremor.

Here, then, is a significant parallel between the workings of the nervous system and of certain machines. The feedback principle introduces an important new idea in nerve physiology. The central nervous system no longer appears to be a self-contained organ receiving signals from the senses and discharging into the muscles. On the contrary, some of its most characteristic activities are explainable only as circular processes, traveling from the nervous system into the muscles and re-entering the nervous system through the sense organs. This finding seems to mark a step forward in the study of the nervous system as an integrated whole.

The new approach represented by cybernetics–an integration of studies which is not strictly biological or strictly physical, but a combination of the two–has already given evidence that it may help to solve many problems in engineering, in physiology and very likely in psychiatry.

This work represents the outcome of a program undertaken jointly several years ago by the writer and Arturo Rosenblueth, then of the Harvard Medical School and now of the National Institute of Cardiology of Mexico. Dr. Rosenblueth is a physiologist; I am a mathematician. For many years Dr. Rosenblueth and I had shared the conviction that the most fruitful areas for the growth of the sciences were those which had been neglected as no-man's lands between the various established fields. Dr. Rosenblueth always insisted that a proper exploration of these blank spaces on the map of science could be made only by a team of scientists, each a specialist but each possessing a thoroughly sound acquaintance with the fields of his fellows.

Our collaboration began as the result of a wartime project. I had been assigned, with a partner, Julian H. Bigelow, to the problem of working out a fire-control apparatus for anti-aircraft artillery which would be capable of tracking the curving course of a plane and predicting its future position. We soon came to the conclusion that any solution of the problem must depend heavily on the feedback principle, as it operated not only in the apparatus but in the human operators of the gun and of the plane. We approached Dr. Rosenblueth with a specific question concerning oscillations in the nervous system, and his reply, which cited the phenomenon of purpose tremor, confirmed our hypothesis about the importance of feedback in voluntary activity.

The ideas suggested by this discussion led to several joint experiments, one of which was a study of feedback in the muscles of cats. The scope of our investigations steadily widened, and as it did so scientists from widely diverse fields joined our group. Among them were the mathematicians John Von Neumann of the Institute for Advanced Study and Walter Pitts of Massachusetts Institute of Technology; the physiologists Warren McCulloch of the University of Pennsylvania and Lorente de No of the Rockefeller Institute; the late Kurt Lewin, psychologist, of M. I. T.; the anthropologists Gregory Bateson and Margaret Mead; the economist Oskar Morgenstern of the Institute for Advanced Study; and others in psychology, sociology, engineering, anatomy, neurophysiology, physics, and so on.

The study of cybernetics is likely to have fruitful applications in many fields, from the design of control mechanisms for artificial limbs to the almost complete mechanization of industry. But in our view it encompasses much wider horizons. If the 17th and early 18th centuries were the age of clocks, and the latter 18th and 19th centuries the age of steam engines, the present time is the age of communication and control. There is in electrical engineering a division which is known as the split between the technique of strong currents and the technique of weak currents; it is this split which separates the age just passed from that in which we are living. What distinguishes communication engineering from power engineering is that the main interest of the former is not the economy of energy but the accurate reproduction of a signal.

At every stage of technique since Daedalus, the ability of the artificer to produce a working simulacrum of a living organism has always intrigued people. In the days of magic, there was the bizarre and sinister concept of the Golem, that figure of clay into which the rabbi of Prague breathed life. In Isaac Newton's time the automaton became the clockwork music box. In the 19th century, the automaton was a glorified heat engine, burning a combustible fuel instead of the glycogen of human muscles. The automaton of our day opens doors by means of photocells, or points guns to the place at which a radar beam picks up a hostile airplane, or computes the solution of a differential equation.

Under the influence of the prevailing view in the science of the 19th century, the engineering of the body was naturally considered to be a branch of power engineering. Even today this is the predominant point of view among classically minded, conservative physiologists. But we are now coming to realize that the body is very far from a conservative system, and that the power available to it is much less limited than was formerly believed. We are beginning to see that such important elements as the neurones–the units of the nervous complex of our bodies–do their work under much the same conditions as vacuum tubes, their relatively small power being supplied from outside by the body's circulation, and that the bookkeeping which is most essential to describe their function is not one of energy.

In short, the newer study of automata, whether in the metal or in the flesh, is a branch of communications engineering, and its cardinal ideas are those of the message, of the amount of disturbance or "noise" (a term taken from the telephone engineer), of the quantity of information to be transmitted, of coding technique, and so on.

This view obviously has implications which affect many branches of science.

Let us consider here the application of cybernetics to the problem of mental disorders. The realization that the brain and computing machines have much in common may suggest new and valid approaches to psychopathology, and even to psychiatry.

These begin with perhaps the simplest question of all: how the brain avoids gross blunders or gross miscarriages of activity due to the malfunction of individual parts. Similar questions referring to the computing machine are of great practical importance, for here a chain of operations, each of which covers only a fraction of a millionth of a second, may last a matter of hours or days. It is quite possible for a chain of computational operations to involve a billion separate steps. Under these circumstances, the chance that at least one operation will go amiss is far from negligible, even though the reliability of modern electronic apparatus has exceeded the most sanguine expectations.

In ordinary computational practice by hand or by desk machines, it is the custom to check every step of the computation and, when an error is found, to localize it by a backward process starting from the first point where the error is noted. To do this with a high-speed machine, the check must proceed at the pace of the original machine, or the whole effective order of speed of the machine will conform to that of the slower process of checking.

A much better method of checking, and in fact the one generally used in practice, is to refer every operation simultaneously to two or three separate mechanisms. When two such mechanisms are used, their answers are automatically collated against each other; and if there is a discrepancy. all data are transferred to permanent storage, the machine stops and a signal is sent to the operator that something is wrong. The operator then compares the results, and is guided by them in his search for the malfunctioning part, perhaps a tube which has burned out and needs replacement. If three separate mechanisms are used for each stage, there will practically always be agreement between two of the three mechanisms, and this agreement will give the required result. In this case the collation mechanism accepts the majority report, and the machine need not stop. There is a signal, however, indicating where and how the minority report differs from the majority report. If this occurs at the first moment of discrepancy, the indication of the position of the error may be very precise.

It is conceivable, and not implausible, that at least two of the elements of this process are also represented in the nervous system. It is hardly to be expected that any important message is entrusted for transmission to a single neurone, or that an important operation is entrusted to a single neuronal mechanism. Like the computing machine, the brain probably works on a variant of the famous principle expounded by Lewis Carroll in *The Hunting of the Snark*: "What I tell you three times is true."

It is also improbable that the various channels available for the transfer of information generally go from one end of their course to the other without connecting with one another. It is much more probable that when a message reaches a certain level of the nervous system, it may leave that point and proceed to the next by one or more alternative routes. There may be parts of the nervous system, especially in the cortex, where this interchangeability is much limited or abolished. Still, the principle holds, and it probably holds most clearly for the relatively unspecialized cortical areas which serve the purpose of association and of what we call the higher mental functions.

So far we have been considering errors in performance that are normal, and pathological only in an extended sense. Let us now turn to those that are much more clearly pathological. Psychopathology has been rather a disappointment to the instinctive materialism of the doctors, who have taken the view that every disorder must be accompanied by actual lesions of some specific tissue involved. It is true that specific brain lesions, such as injuries, tumors, clots and the like, may be accompanied by psychic symptoms, and that certain mental diseases, such as paresis, are the sequelae of general bodily disease and show a pathological condition of the brain tissue. But there is no way of identifying the brain of a schizophrenic of one of the strict Kraepelin types, nor of a manic-depressive patient, nor of a paranoiac. These we call functional disorders.

This distinction between functional and organic disorders is illuminated by the consideration of the computing machine. It is not the empty physical structure of the computing machine that corresponds to the brain–to the adult brain, at least–but the combination of this structure with the instructions given it at the beginning of a chain of operations and with all the additional information stored and gained from outside in the course of its operation. This information is stored in some physical form–in the form of memory. But part of it is in the form of circulating memories, with a physical basis that vanishes when the machine is shut down or the brain dies, and part is in the form of long-time memories, which are stored in a way at which we can only guess, but probably also in a form with a physical basis that vanishes at death.

There is therefore nothing surprising in considering the functional mental disorders fundamentally as diseases of memory, of the circulating information kept by the brain in active state and of the long-time permeability of synapses. Even the grosser disorders such as paresis may produce a large part of their effects not so much by the destruction of tissue which they involve and the alteration of synaptic thresholds as by the secondary disturbances of traffic, the overload of what remains of the nervous system and the rerouting of messages which must follow such primary injuries.

In a system containing a large number of neurones, circular processes can hardly be stable for long periods of time. Either they run their course, dissipate themselves and die out, as in the case of memories belonging to the specious present, or they embrace more and more neurones in their system, until they occupy an inordinate part of the neurone pool. This is what we should expect to be the case in the malignant worry that accompanies anxiety neuroses. In such a case, it is possible that the patient simply does not have the room–i.e., a sufficient number of neurones–to carry out his normal processes of thought. Under such conditions, there may be less going on in the brain to occupy the neurones not yet affected, so that they are all the more readily involved in the expanding process. Furthermore, the permanent memory becomes more and more deeply involved, and the pathological process which began at the level of the circulating memories may repeat itself in a more intractable form at the level of the permanent memories. Thus what started as a relatively trivial and accidental disturbance of stability may build itself up into a process totally destructive to the normal mental life.

Pathological processes of a somewhat similar nature are not unknown in the case of mechanical or electrical computing machines. A tooth of a wheel may slip under such conditions that no tooth with which it engages can pull it back into its normal relations, or a high-speed electrical computing machine may go into a circular process that seems impossible to stop.

How do we deal with these accidents in the case of the machine? We first try to clear the machine of all information, in the hope that when it starts again with different data the difficulty will not recur. If this fails and the difficulty is inaccessible to the clearing mechanism, we shake the machine or, if it is electrical, subject it to an abnormally large electrical impulse in the hope that we may jolt the inaccessible part in to a position where the false cycle of its activities will be interrupted. If even this fails, we may disconnect an erring part of the apparatus, for it is possible that what remains may be adequate for our purpose.

In the case of the brain, there is no normal process, except death, that can clear it of all past impressions. Of the normal non-fatal processes. sleep comes closest to clearing the brain. How often we find that the best way to handle a complicated worry or an intellectual muddle is to sleep on it! Sleep, however, does not clear away the deeper memories, nor indeed is a malignant state of worry compatible with adequate sleep.

Thus we are often forced to resort to more violent types of intervention in the memory cycle. The most violent of these involve surgery on the brain, leaving behind permanent damage, mutilation and the abridgement of the powers of the victim, for the mammalian central nervous system seems to possess no power of regeneration. The principal type of surgical intervention that has been practiced is known as prefrontal lobotomy, or leucotomy. It consists in the removal or isolation of a portion of the prefrontal lobe of the cortex. It is currently having a certain vogue, probably not unconnected with the fact that it makes the custodial care of many patients easier. (Let me remark in passing that killing them makes their custodial care still easier.) Prefrontal lobotomy does seem to have a genuine effect on malignant worry, not by bringing the patient nearer to a solution of his problem, but by damaging or destroying the capacity for maintained worry, known in the terminology of another profession as the conscience. It appears to impair the circulating memory. i.e., the ability to keep in mind a situation not actually presented.

The various forms of shock treatment–electric insulin, metrazol–are less drastic methods of doing a very similar thing. They do not destroy brain tissue, or at least are not intended to destroy it, but they do have a decidedly damaging effect on the memory. In so far as the shock treatment affects recent disordered memories, which are probably scarcely worth preserving anyhow, it has something to recommend it as against lobotomy, but it is sometimes followed by deleterious effects on the permanent memory and the personality. As it is used at present, it is another violent, imperfectly understood, imperfectly controlled method to interrupt a mental vicious circle.

In long-established cases of mental disorder, the permanent memory is as badly deranged as the circulating memory. We do not seem to possess any purely pharmaceutical or surgical weapon for intervening selectively in the permanent memory. This is where psychoanalysis and the other psychotherapeutic measures come in.

Whether psychoanalysis is taken in the orthodox Freudian sense or in the modified senses of Jung and of Adler, or whether the psychotherapy is not strictly psychoanalytic at all, the treatment is clearly based on the concept that the stored information of the mind lies on many levels of accessibility. The effect and accessibility of this stored information are vitally conditioned by affective experiences that we cannot always uncover by introspection. The technique of the psychoanalyst consists in a series of means to discover and interpret these hidden memories, to make the patient accept them for what they are, and thus to modify, if not their content, at least the affective tone they carry, and make them less harmful.

All this is perfectly consistent with the cybernetic point of view. Our theory perhaps explains, too, why there are circumstances in which a joint use of shock treatment and psychotherapy is indicated, combining a physical or pharmacological therapy for the malignant reverberations in the nervous system and a psychological therapy for the damaging long-time memories which might re-establish the vicious circle broken up by the shock treatments.

We have already mentioned the traffic problem of the nervous system. It has been noted by many writers that each form of organization has an upper limit of size beyond which it will not function. Thus insect organization is limited by the length of tubing over which the spiracle method of bringing air by diffusion directly to the breathing tissues will function; a land animal cannot be so big that the legs or other portions in contact with the ground will be crushed by its weight, and so on. The same sort of thing is observed in engineering structures. Skyscrapers are limited in size by the fact that when they exceed a certain height, the elevator space needed for the upper stories consumes an excessive part of the cross section of the lower floors. Beyond a certain span, the best possible suspension bridge will collapse under its own weight. Similarly, the size of a single telephone exchange is limited.

In a telephone system, the important limiting factor is the fraction of the time during which a subscriber will find it impossible to put a call through. A 90 per cent chance of completing calls is probably good enough to permit business to be carried on with reasonable facility. A success of 75 per cent is annoying but will permit business to be carried on after a fashion; if half the calls are not completed, subscribers will begin to ask to have their telephones taken out. Now, these represent all-over figures. If the calls go through a number of distinct stages of switching, and the probability of failure is independent and equal for each stage, in order to get a high probability of final success the probability of success at each stage must be higher than the final one. Thus to obtain a 75 per cent chance for the completion of the call after five stages, we must have about 95 per cent chance of success at each stage. The more stages there are, the more rapidly the service becomes extremely bad when a critical level of failure for the individual call is exceeded, and extremely good when this critical level of failure is not quite reached. Thus a switching service involving many stages and designed for a certain level of failure shows no obvious signs of failure until the traffic comes up to the edge of the critical point, when it goes completely to pieces and we have a catastrophic traffic jam.

So man, with the best developed nervous system of all the animals, probably involving the longest chains of effectively operated neurones, is likely to perform a complicated type of behavior efficiently very close to the edge of an overload, when he will give way in a serious and catastrophic manner. This overload may take place in several ways: by an excess in the amount of traffic to be carried; by a physical removal of channels for the carrying of traffic; or by the excessive occupation of such channels by undesirable systems of traffic, such as circulating memories that have accumulated to the extent of becoming pathological worries. In all these cases, a point is reached–quite suddenly–when the normal traffic does not have space enough allotted to it, and we have a form of mental breakdown, very possibly amounting to insanity.

This will first affect the faculties or operations involving the longest chains of neurones. There is appreciable evidence, of various kinds, that these are precisely the processes recognized as the highest in our ordinary scale of valuation.

If we compare the human brain with that of a lower mammal, we find that it is much more convoluted. The relative thickness of the gray matter is much the same, but it is spread over a far more involved system of grooves and ridges. The effect of this is to increase the amount of gray matter at the expense of the amount of white matter. Within a ridge, this decrease of the white matter is largely a decrease in length rather than in number of fibers, as the opposing folds are nearer together than the same areas would be on a smooth-surfaced brain of the same size. On the other hand, when it comes to the connectors between different ridges, the distance they have to run is increased by the convolution of the brain.

Thus the human brain would seem to be fairly efficient in the matter of the short-distance connectors, but defective in the matter of long-distance trunk lines. This means that in the case of a traffic jam, the processes involving parts of the brain quite remote from one another should suffer first. That is, processes involving several centers, a number of different motor processes and a considerable number of association areas should be among the least stable in cases of insanity. These are precisely the processes which we should normally class as higher, thereby confirming our theory, as experience does also, that the higher processes deteriorate first in insanity.

The phenomena of handedness and of hemispheric dominance suggest other interesting speculations. Righthandedness, as is well known, is generally associated with left-brained ness, and left-handedness with right-brainedness. The dominant hemisphere has the lion's share of the higher cerebral functions. In the adult, the effect of an extensive injury in the secondary hemisphere is far less serious than the effect of a similar injury in the dominant hemisphere. At a relatively early stage in his career, Louis Pasteur suffered a cerebral hemorrhage on the right side which left him with a moderate degree of one-sided paralysis. When he died, his brain was examined and the damage to its right side was found to be so extensive that it has been said that after his injury "he had only half a brain." Nevertheless, after this injury he did some of his best work. A similar injury to the left side of the brain in a righthanded adult would almost certainly have been fatal; at the least it would have reduced the patient to an animal condition.

In the first six months of life, an extensive injury to the dominant hemisphere may compel the normally secondary hemisphere to take its place, so that the patient appears far more nearly normal than he would have been had the injury occurred at a later stage. This is quite in accordance with the great flexibility shown by the nervous system in the early weeks of life. It is possible that, short of very serious injuries, handedness is reasonably flexible in the very young child. Long before the child is of school age, however, the natural handedness and cerebral dominance are established for life. Many people have changed the handedness of their children by education, though of course they could not change its physiological basis in hemispheric dominance. These hemispheric changelings often become stutterers and develop other defects of speech, reading and writing.

We now see at least one possible explanation for this phenomenon. With the education of the secondary hand, there has been a partial education of that part of the secondary hemisphere which deals with skilled motions such as writing. Since these motions are carried out in the closest possible association with reading, and with speech and other activities which are inseparably connected with the dominant hemisphere, the neurone chains involved in these processes must cross over from hemisphere to hemisphere, and in any complex activity they must do this again and again. But the direct connectors between the hemispheres in a brain as large as that of man are so few in number that they are of -very little help. Consequently the interhemispheric traffic must go by roundabout routes through the brain stem. We know little about these routes, but they are certainly long, scanty and subject to interruption. As a consequence, the processes associated with speech and writing are very likely to be involved in a traffic jam, and stuttering is the most natural thing in the world.

The human brain is probably too large already to use in an efficient manner all the facilities which seem to be present. In a cat, the destruction of the dominant hemisphere seems to produce relatively less damage than in man, while the destruction of the secondary hemisphere probably produces more damage. At any rate, the apportionment of function in the two hemispheres is more nearly equal. In man, the gain achieved by the increase in the size and complexity of the brain is partly nullified by the fact that less of the organ can be used effectively at one time.

It is interesting to reflect that we may be facing one of those limitations of nature in which highly specialized organs reach a level of declining efficiency and ultimately lead to the extinction of the species. The human brain may be as far long on its road to destructive specialization as the great nose horns of the last of the titanotheres.

About the Author

Norbert Wiener is professor of mathematics at Massachusetts Institute of Technology.

Collective Computation in Neuronlike Circuits

By David W. Tank and John J. Hopfield

Modern digital computers are latecomers to the world of computation. Biological computers–the brain and nervous system of animals and human beings–have existed for millions of years, and they are marvelously effective in processing sensory information and controlling the interactions of animals with their environment. Tasks such as reaching for a sandwich, recognizing a face or remembering things associated with the taste of madeleines are computations just as much as multiplication and running video games are.

The fact that biological computation is so effective suggests that it may be possible to attain similar capabilities in artificial devices based on the design principles of neural systems. We have studied a number of "neural network" electronic circuits that can carry out significant computations. Such simple models have only a metaphorical resemblance to nature's computers, but they offer an elegant, different way of thinking about machine computation, which is inspiring new microelectronic chip and computer designs. They may also provide fresh insights into the biological systems.

Current research on this subject builds on a long history of efforts to capture the principles of biological computation in mathematical models. The effort began with the pioneering investigations of neurons as logical devices by Warren S. McCulloch and Walter H. Pitts in 1943. In the 1960's Frank Rosenblatt of Cornell University and Bernard Widrow, who is now at Stanford University, created "adaptive neurons" and simple networks that learn. Widrow's Adaline (short for adaptive linear element) is a single-neuron system that can learn to recognize a pattern such as a letter regardless of its orientation or size. Through the 1960's and 1970's a small number of investigators such as Shunichi Amari, Leon N. Cooper, Kunihiko

Fukushima and Stephen Grossberg attempted to model the behavior of real neurons in computational networks more closely and to develop mathematics and architectures for extracting features from patterns, for classifying patterns and for "associative memory," in which pieces of the stored information itself serve to retrieve an entire memory.

The 1980's have seen an extraordinary growth of interest in neural models and their computational properties. Many factors converged to bring this about: neurobiologists were gaining more understanding of how information is processed in nature, cheap computer power made it possible to analyze the models in detail and there was growing interest in parallel computation and analog VLSI (very-large-scale integration), which lend themselves to implementations of neuronlike circuits. New concepts in the mathematics of neural models accompanied these developments. Our work has focused on the principles that give rise to computational behavior in a particular type of neuronlike circuit.

Neurons, or nerve cells, are complex, but even a highly simplified model of a neuron, when it is connected with others in an appropriate network, can do significant computations. A biological neuron receives information from other neurons through synaptic connections and passes on signals to as many as a thousand other neurons. The synapse, or connection between neurons, mediates the "strength" with which a signal crosses from one neuron to another. One can readily build artificial "neural" circuits from simple electronic components: operational amplifiers replace the neurons, and wires, resistors and capacitors replace the synaptic connections. The output voltage of the amplifier represents the activity of the model neuron, and currents through the wires and resistors represent the flow of information in the network.

Strikingly, both the simplified biological model and the artificial network share a common mathematical formulation as a dynamical system–a system of several interacting parts whose state evolves continuously with time. The manner in which a dynamical system evolves depends on the form of the interactions.

In any neural network the interactions result from the effects one "neuron" has on another by virtue of the connection between them. Thus it is not surprising that the behavior of the neural circuits depends critically on the details of the connections. The particular circuits we have studied have connection patterns appropriate for computing solutions to optimization problems, a class of mathematical problems that involve finding a "best solution" from among a very large number of choices.

The computational behavior exhibited by such circuits is a collective property that results from having many computing elements act on one another in a richly interconnected system. The collective properties can be studied using Simplified model neurons, in much the same way as it is possible to understand other large physical systems by greatly reducing the details of their basic components. For example, to study the origin of collective laws of fluid motion, one can simplify the description of complex molecular collisions and produce a tractable model that captures collective features such as temperature and viscosity. Similarly, in seeking to develop a tractable model of the computations carried out by a large number of model neurons, we de-emphasized the details of the processing that goes on at the level of the individual cells and synapses. By simplifying in this way, we were able to discover the general principles by which one can understand collective computation in these circuits.

To comprehend how collective circuits work, it helps to take a very broad view of the essence of computation. Any computing entity, whether it is a digital or analog device or a collection of nerve cells, begins with an initial state and moves through a series of changes to arrive at a state that corresponds to an "answer." The process can be pictured as a path, from initial state to answer, through the physical "configuration space" of the computer as it evolves with time. In a digital computer, for example, the configuration space is defined by the set of voltages for its devices. The input data and program provide initial values for these voltage settings, which change as the computation proceeds and eventually reach a final configuration, which is reported to an output device, such as a screen or a printer.

For any computer there are two critical questions: How does it determine the overall path? And how does it restore itself to that path when physical fluctuations and "noise" cause the computation to drift hopelessly off course? In a digital computer the path is broken down into logical steps that are embodied in the computer's program. In addition, each computing unit protects against voltage fluctuations by treating a range of voltages, rather than just the exact voltage, as being equal to a nominal value; for example, signals between .8 volt and 1.2 volts can all be restored to 1.0 volt after each logical step in the computation.

In collective-decision circuits the process of computation is significantly different. The overall progress of the computation is determined not by step-by-step instructions but by the rich structure of connections among computing devices. Instead of advancing and then restoring the computational path at discrete intervals, the circuit channels or focuses it in one continuous process. These two styles of computation are rather like two different approaches by which a committee makes decisions. In a digital-computer-style committee the members vote yes or no in sequence; each member knows about only a few preceding votes and cannot change a vote once it is cast. In contrast, in a collective-decision committee the members vote together and can express a range of opinions; the members know about all the other votes and can change their opinions. The committee generates a collective decision, or what might be called a sense of the meeting.

The nature of collective computation suggests that it might be particularly effective for problems that involve global interaction between different parts of the problem. We have designed circuits that perform this type of computation to solve certain optimization problems. A typical example is the task-assignment problem, which poses the question: If you have a certain number of assistants and a certain number of tasks, and each assistant does each task at a different rate, how should you assign the tasks so that the corresponding rates add up to the largest total rate? The neural-network circuit that can solve the problem has many interconnected amplifiers that process the data in parallel. It is able to follow the computational path to a solution rapidly. Because this is a rather complicated circuit, it is helpful to first examine some simple circuits that illuminate the basic principles of all such circuits.

The simplest example for the purpose is the flip-flop, a circuit that is widely used in the electronics industry. The circuit has two stable states–which give it its name–and it makes a decision by choosing one state over the other. It can be built from a pair of saturable amplifiers. In such an amplifier the output voltage increases as the input rises until it reaches a saturation level, beyond which it will not change. The reverse is also true: as the input decreases, the output falls until it saturates at a minimum value. In the flip-flop the output of each of the two amplifiers is inverted (that is, multiplied by -1) and connected to the input of the other. The amplifiers mutually inhibit each other because a high output by either one will drive down the input of the other amplifier. This produces a self-consistent pattern, because each amplifier will drive the other one to be in the opposite state. The flip-flop therefore has two stable states: if amplifier *A* is putting out + 1, then *B* will put out -1, and vice versa. The significant feature of this circuit is that the pattern of the connections is the key to its stability and determines the form of its stable states.

A seemingly remarkable feature of the flip-flop is that no matter what initial inputs are supplied to the circuit when it is turned on, it will make a rapid trajectory to one of the stable states. To understand the phenomenon, picture what happens when a raindrop lands on a terrain of hills and valleys. The drop moves generally downhill until it ends up at the bottom of a nearby valley. The path taken is one in which the gravitational potential energy of the raindrop is continuously decreasing. Similarly, the flip-flop's trajectory is associated with a mathematical quantity we call the computational energy *E*, which can be visualized as a terrain on which the flip-flop's voltage state moves continuously downhill.

E is defined by an explicit mathematical formula that depends on the characteristics of the amplifiers, the strength of the excitatory and inhibitory connections between them, and any external inputs. For fixed inputs in a particular circuit, if *E* is calculated for each possible configuration of amplifier voltages, it defines a continuous surface. For the flip-flop *E* can be plotted on a three-dimensional graph. The surface contains two valleys near the voltage configurations (+ 1, -1) and (-1, + 1), which correspond to the two stable states. When the circuit is operating, the changing voltages will describe a downhill motion along the *E* surface, and eventually the circuit's configuration will come to rest at the bottom of one of the valleys.

The concept of the computational energy proves useful in understanding many features of collective-decision circuits. For example, modifications of the flip-flop circuit alter the shape of the *E* surface in well-defined ways. If the strengths of the inhibitory connections increase, the valleys become deeper in relation to the "neutral point," or saddle point, in the middle of the *E* surface. External sources of current also alter the contours of the surface; if a positive current is supplied to the input of one of the amplifiers, it will tend to drive the amplifier to the +1 output state. The valley corresponding to this stable configuration will become deeper, and the change will be accompanied by an increase in the size of the "basin of attraction," the area within which any starting point will settle into the stable state at the bottom of the basin. If the external current is large enough, the basin of attraction will fill the entire flip-flop space, eliminating the valley corresponding to the other stable state and leaving only one stable state for the circuit.

The simple flip-flop circuit illustrates how the process of following the trajectory can be interpreted as a process of decision making. For example, the circuit can decide which of two numbers is larger if the amplifiers are given two external input currents that are proportional to the numbers. The amplifier with the larger input will then have a deeper valley at the stable state for which its output is +1, and its basin of attraction would expand to include the "neutral point." When the computation is begun by setting the voltages at this point, the circuit state would follow a downhill path to the deeper valley. When the circuit stabilizes, one can note which of the two amplifiers is in the +1 state and so determine which number is the larger. For any pair of numbers the corresponding input currents will cause the E surface to change in an appropriate way, thereby ensuring that the path will lead to the correct answer.

For more complicated collective-decision circuits the corresponding E surface acquires so many dimensions that it becomes impossible to draw. Nonetheless, one can understand the general features of the surface and use these as a guide to designing and understanding the circuits. For example, we can generalize from the E surface of the flip-flop to devise a collective-decision circuit that can solve the slightly more difficult problem of determining the largest number in a set of n numbers. The circuit can be thought of as an *n-flop*, consisting of n amplifiers, each of which is connected to all others with inhibitory connections of equal value. It would have n stable states and its E surface would have n valleys. When a set of input currents is supplied to its amplifiers, the deepest valley would develop for the state that has a +1 output for the amplifier receiving the largest input.

In both the flip-flop and the n-flop there is a one-to-one relation between the number of amplifiers and the possible solutions, so that as the number of solutions gets larger, the size of the circuit does too. Is it possible to design a collective circuit that can represent a greater number of solutions than there are amplifiers? Such circuits do indeed exist. They have stable states that consist of *configurations* of amplifiers in the +1 state. This is a more economical use of amplifiers, just as the Roman alphabet is more economical than Chinese ideographs in its use of symbols to encode words.

In 1984 we discovered that networks of this type could rapidly compute good solutions to optimization problems such as the task-assignment problem mentioned above. As an example, imagine you are supervising the job of reshelving books for a large library. You have a number of assistants to do this for you. Each one is familiar with each collection–history, physics and so on–but to varying degrees.

Thus Jessica can shelve six books per minute in geology, four per minute in physics and so on, whereas George can shelve one book per minute in geology, eight per minute in physics and so on. You must assign one category to each assistant. How should you assign the tasks so that the total rate of reshelving the books is as high as possible?

One could attack the problem by brute force, trying out every possible combination in sequence. But if there are many assistants and collections, one would soon be overwhelmed by the number of possibilities. If there are n categories of books and n assistants, the number of possible solutions would be the factorial of n, or $n(n - 1)(n - 2) \ldots 1$. There are better iterative digital-computer algorithms that can arrive at an answer in a time period proportional to n cubed. The computation could be done even faster, however, if one could take full advantage of the problem's essence: the fact that the proper assignment of each worker depends on the capabilities of every other worker. Ideally the mutual dependencies should be considered simultaneously. It is precisely this kind of computation that can be done quickly and efficiently by a collective-decision circuit.

The data in the task-assignment problem consist of the set of shelving rates. These data can be arranged in a table, in which each row contains the rates for an individual assistant and each column represents a book category. An assignment of tasks can then be thought of as the choice of n elements in the table, with the constraint that there can be one and only one element chosen in each row and column, because only one assistant can be assigned to each category. The best solution has the highest sum of rates for the chosen assistants.

We solved the problem by building an n-by-n array of amplifiers in which each row corresponds to an assistant and each amplifier in the row corresponds to a different task. The amplifiers in each row and column are linked by mutually inhibitory connections; this provides the constraint that only one assistant can be assigned to each collection, because if one of the amplifiers has a + 1 output, the other amplifiers are inhibited. Another way of looking at the circuit is that each row and column is an n-flop. These n-flops cannot function independently, however, because each amplifier belongs to two such n-flops. As you will see below, this pattern of connections is the key to the circuit: it ensures that the circuit will have self-consistent stable states that correspond to possible solutions to the problem.

What are the stable states of this network and what does its *E* surface look like? The stable states consist of configurations of 36 amplifiers in which there are six amplifiers with +1 outputs, with one and only one such amplifier in any row or column. In a six-by-six array the number of these stable states is 720, or 6 factorial. The *E* surface for the circuit has valleys of equal depth for each of the 720 possibilities. An input current proportional to the shelving rate of each assistant for each collection is fed to the corresponding amplifier. The valley for each possible solution becomes deeper by an amount proportional to the sum of its corresponding shelving rates.

The network carries out the computation by following a trajectory down the *E* surface. In the final configuration the circuit usually settles into the deepest valley, which is the correct choice because it corresponds to the task assignment that has the highest total shelving rate. In simulation studies we have shown that this particular circuit will almost always find the best solution to the problem, and a slightly more complex circuit will always find the best solution.

One reason we are interested in studying this type of circuit is that perceptual problems can often be expressed as an optimization. Our senses gather a large set of information about the external world-information that is inevitably imprecise and "noisy." The edge of an object might be hidden behind another object, for example. We know, however, that the edges of objects are continuous, and just because we cannot see an edge does not make us wonder whether the object has changed its shape. Our interpretation of the information is constrained by what we already know.

This knowledge can often be represented as a set of constraints, similar to those in the task-assignment problem, and express it in an *E* function. The perceptual problem then becomes equivalent to finding the deepest valley in the *E* surface. For example, Cristof Koch, Jose Marroquin and Alan Yuille, who were then at the Massachusetts

Institute of Technology, showed how several important problems in computer vision could be cast as an optimization problem and solved by a collective-decision circuit in which knowledge of the real world had been imposed as a set of constraints. Their circuit was able to take incomplete depth information of a three-dimensional world and reconstruct missing information such as the locations of the edges of objects.

Another particularly interesting application for collective-decision circuits is associative memory, which is a form of optimization problem. An associative memory is different in principle from a digital-computer memory. A conventional computer stores information by assigning addresses, which identify the physical locations where the data will be stored in hardware, such as a sector or track on a floppy disk. When the central processor requires a piece of data, it issues an instruction to read the data at a particular address. The address itself contains no information about the nature of the data stored there.

Now reflect for a moment about your own memories. If you think of a particular friend, you will remember any facts–name, age, hair color, height, job, hobbies, schooling, family, house, shared experiences and so forth. These facts are somehow combined to form your memory of the individual. There is no notion of storage address in the way you retrieve such information from your memory. Instead pieces of the information itself are used in place of an address.

Associative memory is an idea that came from psychology, not electrical engineering. Fruit flies and garden slugs have associative memories. Indeed, the fact that such relatively simple nervous systems display the phenomenon suggests that it must be a natural–almost spontaneous–property of neuron ensembles. It seems reasonable to ask whether associative memory could also be achieved in networks of artificial neuronlike devices. In the 1970's a number of investigators, including James A. Anderson of Brown University and Teuvo Kohonen of the University of Helsinki, developed mathematical models of associative memory.

The concept of the E surface provides a means to understand and study associative-memory circuits built of saturable amplifiers.

How would one make a collective-decision circuit behave like an associative memory? Consider a space of many Cartesian coordinates in which each axis is labeled with some attribute a person might have. One axis might refer to height, one to hair color, one to weight, one to sailing experience, one to the first name of the individual, one to city of residence and so on. Any point in the space describes the characteristics of a hypothetical possible individual. Each of your friends is represented by a particular point in the space. Because you have very few friends compared with the set of all possible individuals, if you put a mark at the position of each of the people you know, you will have marked a very few points in a large space. When someone gives you partial information about a person–for example color of hair and weight but not name–this describes an approximate location in the space of possible people. The idea of an associative memory is to find the friend who best matches the partial data.

A collective-decision circuit such as the one described for the task-assignment problem could perform as an associative memory if the E surface can be shaped to have valleys, or stable points, at the places that correspond to particular memories. A pattern of input voltages corresponding to a partial memory would be supplied to the amplifiers and the circuit would then follow a trajectory to the bottom of a local valley in the E terrain and read out the output state of the amplifiers as the stored memory. Unlike the task-assignment circuit, in which the connections are highly regular because of the simple global rules that constrain the problem, in an associative memory the connections are irregular and the stable points are scattered somewhat at random because the memories need not have any particular relationship among themselves. To construct an associative memory, therefore, one must find connections between amplifiers such that the many desired memories are represented simultaneously by the circuit's stable states.

A simple associative memory of six interconnected amplifiers illustrates how information can be stored in such a network. The memory states of the system could be described as six-bit binary words, in which each bit corresponds to one of the two possible saturated output states of an amplifier, + 1 and -1. For example, memory *A* is (+1, +1,+1, -1,-1, -1). As with the flip-flop circuit, a state can be stable only if it is self-consistent. This is accomplished by ensuring that each amplifier with a +1 output has an excitatory connection to the input of every other amplifier that has a +1 output and an inhibitory connection to the input of each amplifier that has a -1 output, and vice versa for amplifiers that have -1 outputs. All the inputs to an amplifier are added up to give a big signal with the correct sign. If one looks at the E surface for this associative memory, one will find that the connections have created a valley at the location of the memory.

Because the data are distributed in the pattern of the connections in the circuit, many other memories can be overlaid in the same circuit. It is merely necessary to calculate the connections separately for each memory and add them to the connections for the memories already in storage. This simple additive rule works quite effectively as long as not too many of the same connections are shared among many memories. Problems arise if memories are too similar or too numerous; the valleys on the *E* surface get too close and begin to interact. (The number of unrelated memories that can be stored effectively is about 15 percent of the number of "neurons" in the circuit.) There are cleverer schemes that can store a larger number of memories or memories that are more similar.

The associative memory described above requires only local information about two linked "neurons" in order to modify the strength of the existing connection between them. This is appealing because it offers a theory of associative memory that is consistent with a biological model proposed more than 30 years ago by Donald O. Hebb. Hebb postulated that biological associative memory must reside in the synaptic connections between nerve cells and that the process of learning and memory storage involves changes in the strength with which nerve signals are transmitted across individual synapses. According to his theory, synapses linking pairs of neurons that are simultaneously active become stronger, thereby reinforcing those pathways in the brain that are excited by specific experiences. As in our associative-memory model, this involves local instead of global changes in the connections. The Hebbian synapse had long eluded actual observation, but recently several investigators have reported evidence for such mechanisms in the brain.

Many laboratories are now exploring how to fabricate and use devices for collective computation. A variety of prototypes have already been built with microelectronic and optical hardware. To be useful, circuits will have to be large, with hundreds or thousands of "neurons," and because these may be densely interconnected, the circuits may contain tens of thousands or even millions of connections. In addition, in order to build a general-purpose circuit such as an associative-memory chip one would need a simple method for modifying the connection strengths.

John J. Lambe and his collaborators at the Jet Propulsion Laboratory constructed from integrated-circuit amplifiers the first associative-memory network of the type we have described. The connections between each pair of amplifiers were chosen through a mechanical switch. The network was expanded to contain 32 amplifiers, with microcomputer-controlled transistor switches replacing the mechanical ones. These pioneering circuits work as predicted but are too cumbersome to be of practical use. The first VLSI version was fabricated by Massimo Sivilotti, Michael R. Emerling and Carver A. Mead of the California Institute of Technology. The circuit reduced a 22-amplifier network with 462 interconnections to an area smaller than a square centimeter. The chip functioned as an associative memory when the connection matrix was appropriately programmed. Similar VLSI circuits with 54 amplifiers have been built by Lawrence D. Jackel, Richard E. Howard and Hans Peter Graf of the AT&T Bell Laboratories. One of the attractive features of collective-decision circuits is that they converge on a good solution rapidly, typically in a few multiples of the characteristic response time of the computing devices. In several of the microelectronic implementations this convergence has occurred in less than one microsecond. Mead's group has recently built a VLSI "artificial retina" chip for image processing, using collective-computation principles in the design.

Advanced optics provides another promising medium for building collective-decision circuits. In that approach light beams would replace the wires. Because light beams can pass through one another without interaction, this raises the possibility of implementing complicated network topologies that might be difficult to achieve in VLSI. Demetri Psaltis of Caltech and Nabil Farhat of the University of Pennsylvania have built working prototypes of optical collective circuits.

Many investigators are studying neuronlike circuits different from the ones we have described. A popular model is the feedforward Perceptron, which has been shown to be effective for a broad range of applications, such as pattern recognition. This model consists of simple processing units arranged in several layers. Information is passed into the network through an input layer, and the result of the network's computation is read out at the output layer. There are connections between the layers, and information flows forward only. Such feedforward networks have simplified dynamical behavior and reduced computational capability. On the other hand, many useful learning rules have been devised for such circuits that make it easy to find the appropriate connection pattern. One well-known example, called back-propagation, has been independently derived by David Parker, by David Rumelhart, Geoffrey Hinton and Ronald Williams, and by Paul J. Werbos. One goal of current research is to understand how similar learning algorithms might be applied to networks that have the richer dynamical behavior produced by the kind of feedback employed in the circuits we have discussed.

The study of collective computation in neuronlike circuits has shown that such networks can carry out computations that are not trivial. Computations that are more complicated may require having many simple decisions interact collectively to produce a complex decision. Another feature of many complex decisions is that they must combine information arriving over an extended period of time. Suppose, for example, one wants to identify someone from a distance by the way he walks. One must first make simple decisions about the positions of limbs, combine these over time to determine a sequence of movements and from these form a complex pattern that can be associated with a particular individual. The study of such hierarchical and time-varying collective-decision systems has just begun, but we believe that, as in the case of the circuit-design principles we have described, the research will be propelled by the architectures and design rules of nature's computers.

Section 2: The Deep Learning Revolution

How to Teach Computers to Learn on Their Own

By Yaser S. Abu-Mostafa

A couple of years ago the directors of a women's clothing company asked me to help them develop better fashion recommendations for their clients. No one in their right mind would seek my personal advice in an area I know so little about—I am, after all, a male computer scientist—but they were not asking for my personal advice. They were asking for my machine-learning advice, and I obliged. Based purely on sales figures and client surveys, I was able to recommend to women whom I have never met fashion items I have never seen. My recommendations beat the performance of professional stylists. Mind you, I still know very little about women's fashion.

Machine learning is a branch of computer science that enables computers to learn from experience, and it is everywhere. It makes Web searches more relevant, blood tests more accurate and dating services more likely to find you a potential mate. At its simplest, machine-learning algorithms take an existing data set, comb through it for patterns, then use these patterns to generate predictions about the future. Yet advances in machine learning over the past decade have transformed the field. Indeed, machine-learning techniques are responsible for making computers "smarter" than humans at so many of the tasks we wish to pursue. Witness Watson, the IBM computer system that used machine learning to beat the best *Jeopardy* players in the world.

The most important machine-learning competition did not involve talking *Jeopardy*-playing machines, however. A few years ago Netflix, the online movie rental company, wanted to help its customers find movies that they would love—especially films that were not high-demand "new release" titles but rather from their largely ignored back catalogue. The company already had an in-house movie recommendation system, but executives knew it was far from perfect.

So the company launched a competition to improve on existing efforts. The rules were simple: the first entry to beat the performance of the in-house system by 10 percent would earn a $1-million prize. Tens of thousands of people from around the world signed up.

For a machine-learning researcher, the competition was a dream (and not just for the prize money, attractive though it was). The most critical components of any machine-learning system are the data, and the Netflix prize offered 100 million points of real data, ready to download.

Training Days

The Netflix competition lasted for almost three years. Many groups attacked the problem by breaking down individual movies into long arrays of different attributes. For example, you could score any movie on various traits, such as how funny it is, how complicated it is or how attractive the actors are. For each viewer, you go back and take a look at the movies he has reviewed to see how much he values each of these attributes—how much he enjoys comedy, whether he prefers simple or complicated plots, and how much he likes to look at attractive movie stars.

Now prediction becomes a simple matter of matching the viewer's tastes to the new movie's attributes. If he loves comedies and complex plots, chances are he might like a knotty caper such as *Some Like It Hot* or *A Fish Called Wanda*. After the algorithm matches dozens of these attributes, the final recommendation should be a good predictor of how the viewer will like the movie.

We naturally think in easily identifiable attributes such as "comedy" or "complex plot," but algorithms need make no such distinctions. In fact, the entire process is automated—researchers never bother with analyzing movie content. The machine-learning algorithm will start with random, nameless attributes. As it gets data about how viewers rated movies in the past, it fine-tunes attributes until they correspond to how viewers rate movies.

For example, if people who like movie A also tend to like movies B, C and D, the algorithm will come up with a new attribute that is common to A, B, C and D. This happens in the so-called training phase, where the computer searches through millions of viewer ratings. The goal of this phase is to create a set of objective attributes that are based on actual ratings, not on subjective analysis.

It may be hard to interpret the different attributes that the machine-learning algorithm produces; they may not be as straightforward as "comedy content." In fact, they can be quite subtle, even incomprehensible, because the algorithm is only trying to find the best way to predict how a viewer would rate a movie, not necessarily explain to us how it is done. If a system performs well, we do not insist on understanding how it does so.

This is not the way the world is used to operating. Early in my career I developed a credit-approval system for a bank. When I was done, the bank wanted me to interpret what each attribute meant. The request had nothing to do with the system's performance, which was fine. The reason was legal: banks cannot deny credit to someone without articulating a rationale, and they cannot just send a letter to someone saying that the application was denied because *X* is less than 0.5.

Different machine-learning systems will develop unique sets of attributes. In the final weeks of the Netflix competition, groups that had been working independently began to blend their algorithms using so-called aggregation techniques. In the final hour of the three-year competition, two teams were still fighting for the top prize. The scoreboard showed a slight edge to The Ensemble, a team that included a Ph.D. alumnus of my research group at the California Institute of Technology, over BellKor's Pragmatic Chaos. Yet the final audited tally put the teams in a statistical dead heat–each achieved a 10.06 percent improvement over the original algorithm. According to the rules of the competition, in the event of a tie the award would go to the team that submitted its solution first. After three years of competition and in the last hour of battle, BellKor's Pragmatic Chaos submitted its solution 20 minutes earlier than The

Ensemble. A 20-minute delay in a three-year competition made a difference of a million bucks.

The Perfect Fit

The type of machine learning used in the movie-rating competition is called supervised learning. It is also used in tasks such as medical diagnosis. For example, we could provide a computer with thousands of images of white blood cells from patients' historical records, along with information about whether each image is of a cancerous or noncancerous cell. From this information, the algorithm will learn to apply certain cell attributes–shape, size and color, perhaps–to identify malignant cells. Here the researcher "supervises" the learning process. For each image in the training data, he or she gives the computer the correct answer.

Supervised learning is the most common type of machine learning, but it is not the only one. Roboticists, for example, may not know the best way to make a two-legged robot walk. In that case, they could design an algorithm that experiments with a number of different gaits. If a particular gait makes the robot fall down, the algorithm learns to not do that any more.

This is the reinforcement-learning approach. It is basically trial and error–a learning strategy we are all familiar with. In a typical reinforcement-learning scenario–human or machine–we face a situation in which some action is needed. Instead of someone telling us what to do, we try something and see what happens. Based on what happens, we reinforce the good actions and avoid the bad actions in the future. Eventually both we and the machines learn the correct actions for different situations.

For example, consider Internet search engines. The founders of Google did not wade through the Web circa 1997 to train its computers to recognize pages about, say, "Dolly the sheep." Instead their algorithms crawled the Web to generate a first draft of results, then they relied on user clicks to reinforce which pages were relevant and which were not. When users click on a page link in the search results, the machine-learning algorithm learns that the page is relevant. If users ignore a link that appears at the top of the search results, the algorithm infers that the page is not relevant. The algorithm combines such feedback from millions of users to adjust how it evaluates pages in future searches.

Excess Problems

Researchers often use reinforcement learning for tasks that require a sequence of actions, such as playing a game. Consider a simple example, like tic-tac-toe. The computer may start by randomly putting an X in a corner. This is a strong move, and the computer will go on to win these games more often than the games that it opens by placing an X on a side. The action that leads to a win–X in the corner–gets reinforced. Researchers then extend this process to infer what the correct action would be at any future step of the game–and for any game, from checkers to Go. Reinforcement learning is also used in advanced economics applications, such as finding a Nash equilibrium.

Sometimes even reinforcement learning is too much to ask for, because we are unable to get feedback on our actions. In such cases, we must turn to "unsupervised learning." Here the researcher has a set of data but no information about what action should be taken–either explicitly, as in supervised learning, or implicitly, as in reinforcement learning. How could we possibly learn from these data? A first step to making sense of it is to categorize the data into groups based on similarity. This is called clustering. It collects unlabeled data and infers information about their hidden structure. Clustering provides us with a better understanding of the data before we consider what action should be taken. Sometimes clustering is enough–if we want to organize a library, simply grouping books into similar categories is all we need to do. At other times, we might go further and apply supervised learning to the clustered data.

Ironically, the biggest trap that machine-learning practitioners fall into is to throw too much computing power at a problem.

Recognizing this fact and being able to deal with it properly are what separate the professionals from the amateurs.

How can more power hurt? Machine-learning algorithms try to detect patterns in the data. If the algorithm is too aggressive—perhaps using too sophisticated a model to fit a limited data sample—it may mislead itself by detecting spurious patterns that happen by coincidence in a sample but do not reflect a true association. A significant part of the research on the mathematical theory of machine learning focuses on this problem of "overfitting" the data. We want to detect genuine connections that fit the data, but we do not want to overdo it and end up picking patterns that cannot be trusted.

To understand how this can happen, imagine a gambler at a roulette table (for the sake of simplicity, we will assume this table has only red and black numbers and does not include 0 or 00). She watches 10 consecutive spins alternate between red and black. "The wheel must be biased," she thinks. "It always goes red, black, red, black, red, black." The player has created a model in her head that the limited data set has confirmed. Yet on the 11th roll, right after she puts down $100 on red, the random nature of the wheel reasserts itself. The wheel stops at black for the second consecutive time, and she loses it all.

Our gambler was looking for a pattern where none really exists. Statistically, any roulette table has about a one in 500 chance of randomly flip-flopping between red and black 10 times in a row. In roulette, however, past spins have no bearing on the future. The next spin always has a 50 percent chance of coming up red. In machine learning, we have an old saying: if you torture the data long enough, it will confess.

To avoid this outcome, machine-learning algorithms are biased to keep the models as simple as possible using a technique called regularization. The more complex a model is, the more prone it is to overfitting; regularization keeps that complexity in check.

Researchers will also commonly validate the algorithm on data that are not in the training set. In this way, we ensure that the performance we are getting is genuine, not just an artifact of the training data. The Netflix prize, for instance, was not judged against the original data set provided to the participants. It was tested on a new data set known only to the people at Netflix.

Predicting the Future

It is difficult to get bored if you work in machine learning. You never know what application you could be working on next. Machine learning enables nonexperts in an application area–computer scientists in women's fashion, for example–to learn and predict based merely on data. As a consequence, interest in the field is exploding. This past spring students from 15 different majors took my machine-learning course at Caltech. For the first time, I also posted course materials online and broadcast live videos of the lectures; thousands of people from around the world watched and completed the assignments.

Machine learning, however, works only for problems that have enough data. Anytime I am presented with a possible machine-learning project, my first question is simple: What data do you have? Machine learning does not create information; it gets the information from the data. Without enough training data that contain proper information, machine learning will not work.

Yet data for myriad fields are becoming ever more abundant, and with them the value of machine learning will continue to rise. Trust me on this–predictions are my specialty.

Referenced

Machines That Learn from Hints. Yaser S. Abu-Mostafa in *Scientific American*, Vol. 272, No. 4, pages 6469; April 1995.

Recommend a Movie, Win a Million Bucks. Joseph Sill in *Engineering & Science*, Vol. 73, No. 2, pages 3239; Spring 2010.

Learning from Data. Yaser S. Abu-Mostafa, Malik Magdon-Ismail and Hsuan-Tien Lin. AMLbook, 2012. http://amlbook.com

Learning from Data (online course): http://work.caltech.edu/telecourse.html

About the Author

Yaser S. Abu-Mostafa is a professor of electrical engineering and computer science at the California Institute of Technology.

Springtime for AI: The Rise of Deep Learning

By Yoshua Bengio

Computers generated a great deal of excitement in the 1950s when they began to beat humans at checkers and to prove math theorems. In the 1960s the hope grew that scientists might soon be able to replicate the human brain in hardware and software and that "artificial intelligence" would soon match human performance on any task. In 1967 Marvin Minsky of the Massachusetts Institute of Technology, who died earlier this year, proclaimed that the challenge of AI would be solved within a generation.

That optimism, of course, turned out to be premature. Software designed to help physicians make better diagnoses and networks modeled after the human brain for recognizing the contents of photographs failed to live up to their initial hype. The algorithms of those early years lacked sophistication and needed more data than were available at the time. Computer processing was also too tepid to power machines that could perform the massive calculations needed to approximate something approaching the intricacies of human thought.

By the mid-2000s the dream of building machines with human-level intelligence had almost disappeared in the scientific community. At the time, even the term "AI" seemed to leave the domain of serious science. Scientists and writers describe the dashed hopes of the period from the 1970s until the mid-2000s as a series of "AI winters."

What a difference a decade makes. Beginning in 2005, AI's outlook changed spectacularly. That was when deep learning, an approach to building intelligent machines that drew inspiration from brain science, began to come into its own. In recent years deep learning has become a singular force propelling AI research forward. Major information technology companies are now pouring billions of dollars into its development.

Deep learning refers to the simulation of networks of neurons that gradually "learn" to recognize images, understand speech or even make decisions on their own. The technique relies on so-called artificial neural networks–a core element of current AI research. Artificial neural networks do not mimic precisely how actual neurons work. Instead they are based on general mathematical principles that allow them to learn from examples to recognize people or objects in a photograph or to translate the world's major languages.

The technology of deep learning has transformed AI research, reviving lost ambitions for computer vision, speech recognition, natural-language processing and robotics. The first products rolled out in 2012 for understanding speech–you may be familiar with Google Now. And shortly afterward came applications for identifying the contents of an image, a feature now incorporated into the Google Photos search engine.

Anyone frustrated by clunky automated telephone menus can appreciate the dramatic advantages of using a better personal assistant on a smartphone. And for those who remember how poor object recognition was just a few years ago–software that might mistake an inanimate object for an animal–strides in computer vision have been incredible: we now have computers that, under certain conditions, can recognize a cat, a rock or faces in images almost as well as humans. AI software, in fact, has now become a familiar fixture in the lives of millions of smartphone users. Personally, I rarely type messages anymore. I often just speak to my phone, and sometimes it even answers back.

These advances have suddenly opened the door to further commercialization of the technology, and the excitement only continues to grow. Companies compete fiercely for talent, and Ph.D.s specializing in deep learning are a rare commodity that is in extremely high demand. Many university professors with expertise in this area–by some counts, the majority–have been pulled from academia to industry and furnished with well-appointed research facilities and ample compensation packages.

Working through the challenges of deep learning has led to stunning successes. The triumph of a neural network over top-ranked player Lee Se-dol at the game of Go received prominent headlines. Applications are already expanding to encompass other fields of human expertise—and it is not all games. A newly developed deep-learning algorithm is purported to diagnose heart failure from magnetic resonance imaging as well as a cardiologist.

Intelligence, Knowledge and Learning

Why did AI hit so many roadblocks in previous decades? The reason is that most of the knowledge we have of the world around us is not formalized in written language as a set of explicit tasks—a necessity for writing any computer program. That is why we have not been able to directly program a computer to do many of the things that we humans do so easily—be it understanding speech, images or language or driving a car. Attempts to do so—organizing sets of facts in elaborate databases to imbue computers with a facsimile of intelligence—have met with scant success.

That is where deep learning comes in. It is part of the broader AI discipline known as machine learning, which is based on principles used to train intelligent computing systems—and to ultimately let machines teach themselves. One of these tenets relates to what a human or machine considers a "good" decision. For animals, evolutionary principles dictate decisions should be made that lead to behaviors that optimize chances of survival and reproduction. In human societies, a good decision might include social interactions that bring status or a sense of well-being. For a machine, such as a self-driving car, though, the quality of decision making depends on how closely the autonomous vehicle imitates the behaviors of competent human drivers.

The knowledge needed to make a good decision in a particular context is not necessarily obvious in a way that can be translated into computer code. A mouse, for instance, has knowledge of its surroundings and an innate sense of where to sniff and how to move its legs, find food or mates, and avoid predators. No programmer would be capable of specifying a step-by-step set of instructions to produce these behaviors. Yet that knowledge is encoded in the rodent's brain.

Before creating computers that can train themselves, computer scientists needed to answer such fundamental questions as how humans acquire knowledge. Some knowledge is innate, but most is learned from experience. What we know intuitively cannot be turned into a clear sequence of steps for a computer to execute but can often be learned from examples and practice. Since the 1950s researchers have looked for and tried to refine general principles that allow animals or humans–or even machines, for that matter–to acquire knowledge through experience. Machine learning aims to establish procedures, called learning algorithms, that allow a machine to learn from examples presented to it.

The science of machine learning is largely experimental because no universal learning algorithm exists–none can enable the computer to learn every task it is given well. Any knowledge-acquisition algorithm needs to be tested on learning tasks and data specific to the situation at hand, whether it is recognizing a sunset or translating English into Urdu. There is no way to prove that it will be consistently better across the board for any given situation than all other algorithms.

AI researchers have fashioned a formal mathematical description of this principle–the "no free lunch" theorem–that demonstrates that no algorithm exists to address every real-world learning situation. Yet human behavior apparently contradicts this theorem. We appear to hold in our head fairly general learning abilities that allow us to master a multitude of tasks for which evolution did not prepare our ancestors: playing chess, building bridges or doing research in AI.

These capabilities suggest that human intelligence exploits general assumptions about the world that might serve as inspiration for creating machines with a form of general intelligence. For just this reason, developers of artificial neural networks have adopted the brain as a rough model for designing intelligent systems.

The brain's main units of computation are cells called neurons. Each neuron sends a signal to other neurons through tiny gaps between the cells known as synaptic clefts. The propensity of a neuron to send a signal across the gap–and the amplitude of that signal–is referred to as synaptic strength. As a neuron "learns," its synaptic strength grows, and it is more likely, when stimulated by an electrical impulse, to send messages along to its neighbors.

Brain science influenced the emergence of artificial neural networks that used software or hardware to create virtual neurons. Early researchers in this subfield of AI, known as connectionism, postulated that neural networks would be able to learn complex tasks by gradually altering the connections among neurons, so that patterns of neural activity would capture the content of its input, such as an image or a snippet of dialogue. As these networks would receive more examples, the learning process would continue by changing synaptic strengths among the connected neurons to achieve more accurate representations of, say, images of a sunset.

Lessons about Sunsets

The current generation of neural networks extends the pioneering work of connectionism. The networks gradually change numerical values for each synaptic connection, values representing the strength of that connection and thus how likely a neuron is to transmit a signal along to another neuron. An algorithm used by deep-learning networks changes these values ever so slightly each time it observes a new image. The values inch steadily closer toward ones that allow the neural network to make better predictions about the image's content. For best results, current learning algorithms require close involvement by a human. Most of these algorithms use supervised learning in which each training example is accompanied by a human-crafted label about what is being learned–a picture of a sunset, say, is associated with a caption that says "sunset." In this instance, the goal of the supervised learning algorithm is to take a photograph as the input and produce, as an output, the name of a key object in the image. The mathematical process of transforming an input to an output is called a function. The numerical values, such as synaptic strengths, that produce this function correspond to a solution to the learning task.

Learning by rote to produce correct answers would be easy but somewhat useless. We want to teach the algorithm what a sunset is but then to have it recognize an image of any sunset, even one it has not been trained on. The ability to discern any sunset–in other words, to generalize learning beyond specific examples–is the main goal of any machine-learning algorithm. In fact, the quality of training of any network is evaluated by testing it using examples not previously seen. The difficulty of generalizing correctly to a new example arises because there is an almost infinite set of possible variations that still correspond to any category, such as a sunset.

To succeed in generalizing from having observed a multitude of examples, the learning algorithm used in deep-learning networks needs more than just the examples themselves. It also relies on hypotheses about the data and assumptions about what a possible solution to a particular problem might be. A typical hypothesis built into the software might postulate that if data inputs for a particular function are similar, the outputs should not radically change–altering a few pixels in an image of a cat should not usually transform the animal into a dog.

One type of neural network that incorporates hypotheses about images is called a convolutional neural network; it has become a key technology that has fueled the revival of AI. Convolutional neural networks used in deep learning have many layers of neurons organized in such a way as to make the output less sensitive to the main object in an image changing, such as whenits position is moved slightly–a well-trained network may be able to recognize a face from different angles in separate photographs. The design of a convolutional network draws its inspiration from the multilayered structure of the visual cortex–the part of our brain that receives input from the eyes. The many layers of virtual neurons in a convolutional neural network are what makes a network "deep" and thus better able to learn about the world around it.

Going Deep

On a practical level, the advances that enabled deep learning came from specific innovations that emerged about 10 years ago, when interest in AI and neural networks had reached its lowest point in decades. A Canadian organization funded by the government and private donors, the Canadian Institute for Advanced Research (CIFAR), helped to rekindle the flame by sponsoring a program led by Geoffrey Hinton of the University of Toronto. The program also included Yann LeCun of New York University, Andrew Ng of Stanford University, Bruno Olshausen of the University of California, Berkeley, me and several others. Back then, negative attitudes toward this line of research made it difficult to publish and even to convince graduate students to work in this area, but a few of us had the strong sense that it was important to move ahead.

Skepticism about neural networks at that time stemmed, in part, from the belief that training them was hopeless because of the challenges involved in optimizing how they behave. Optimization is a branch of mathematics that tries to find the configuration of a set of parameters to reach a mathematical objective. The parameters, in this case, are called synaptic weights and represent how strong a signal is being sent from one neuron to another.

The objective is to make predictions with the minimum number of errors. When the relation between parameters and an objective is simple enough—more precisely when the objective is a convex function of the parameters—the parameters can be gradually adjusted. This continues until they get as close as possible to the values that produce the best possible choice, known as a global minimum—which corresponds to the lowest possible average prediction error made by the network.

In general, however, training a neural network is not so simple—and requires what is called a nonconvex optimization. This type of optimization poses a much greater challenge—and many researchers believed that the hurdle was insurmountable. The learning algorithm can get stuck in what is called a local minimum, in which it is unable to reduce the prediction error of the neural network by adjusting parameters slightly.

Only in the past year was the myth dispelled that neural networks were hard to train because of local minima. We found in our research that when a neural network is sufficiently large, the local minima problem is greatly reduced. Most local minima actually correspond to having learned knowledge at a level that almost matches the optimal value of the global minimum.

Although the theoretical problems of optimization could, in theory, be solved, building large networks with more than two or three layers had often failed. Beginning in 2005, CIFAR-supported efforts achieved breakthroughs that overcame these barriers. In 2006 we managed to train deeper neural networks, using a technique that proceeded layer by layer.

Later, in 2011, we found a better way to train even deeper networks–ones with more layers of virtual neurons–by altering the computations performed by each of these processing units, making them more like what biological neurons actually compute. We also discovered that injecting random noise into the signals transmitted among neurons during training, similar to what happens in the brain, made them better able to learn to correctly identify an image or sound.

Two crucial factors aided the success of deep-learning techniques. An immediate 10-fold increase in computing speed, thanks to the graphics-processing units initially designed for video games, allowed larger networks to be trained in a reasonable amount of time. Also fueling deep learning's growth was the availability of huge labeled data sets for which a learning algorithm can identify the correct answer–"cat," for example, when inspecting an image in which a cat is just one element.

Another reason for deep learning's recent success is its ability to learn to perform a sequence of computations that construct or analyze, step by step, an image, a sound or other data. The depth of the network is the number of such steps. Many visual- or auditory-recognition tasks in which AI excels require the many layers of a deep network. In recent theoretical and experimental studies, in fact, we have shown that carrying out some of these mathematical operations cannot be accomplished efficiently without sufficiently deep networks.

Each layer in a deep neural network transforms its input and produces an output that is sent to the next layer. The network represents more abstract concepts at its deeper layers, which are more remote from the initial raw sensory input. Experiments show that artificial neurons in deeper layers in the network tend to correspond to more abstract semantic concepts: a visual object such as a desk, for instance. Recognition of the image of the desk might emerge from the processing of neurons at a deeper layer even though the concept of "desk" was not among the category labels on which the network was trained. And the concept of a desk might itself only be an intermediate step toward creating a still more abstract concept at a still higher layer that might be categorized by the network as an "office scene."

Beyond Pattern Recognition

Until recently, artificial neural networks distinguished themselves in large part for their ability to carry out tasks such as recognizing patterns in static images. But another type of neural network is also making its mark–specifically, for events that unfold over time. Recurrent neural networks have demonstrated the capacity to correctly perform a sequence of computations, typically for speech, video and other data. Sequential data are made up of units–whether a phoneme or a whole word–that follow one another sequentially. The way recurrent neural networks process their inputs bears a resemblance to how the brain works. Signals that course among neurons change constantly as inputs from the senses are processed. This internal neural state changes in a way that depends on the current input to the brain from its surroundings before issuing a sequence of commands that result in body movements directed at achieving a specific goal.

Recurrent networks can predict what the next word in a sentence will be, and this can be used to generate new sequences of words, one at a time. They can also take on more sophisticated tasks. After "reading" all the words in a sentence, the network can guess at the meaning of the entire sentence. A separate recurrent network can then use the semantic processing of the first network to translate the sentence into another language.

Research on recurrent neural networks had its own lull in the late 1990s and early 2000s. My theoretical work suggested that they would run into difficulty learning to retrieve information from the far past—the earliest elements in the sequence being processed. Think of trying to recite the words from the first sentences of a book verbatim when you have just reached the last page. But several advances have lessened some of these problems by enabling such networks to learn to store information so that it persists for an extended time. The neural networks can use a computer's temporary memory to process multiple, dispersed pieces of information, such as ideas contained in different sentences spread across a document.

The strong comeback for deep neural networks after the long AI winter is not just a technological triumph. It also provides a lesson in the sociology of science. In particular, it underscores the need to support ideas that challenge the technological status quo and to encourage a diverse research portfolio that backs disciplines that temporarily fall out of favor.

Referenced

ImageNet Classification with Deep Convolutional Neural Networks. Alex Krizhevsky et al. Presented at the 26th Annual Conference on Neural Information Processing Systems (NIPS 2012), Stateline, Nev., December 3–8, 2012.

Representation Learning: A Review and New Perspectives. Y. Bengio et al. in *IEEE Transactions on Pattern Analysis and Machine Intelligence*, Vol. 35, No. 8, pages 1798–1828; August 2013.

Deep Learning. Yann LeCun et al. in *Nature*, Vol. 521, pages 436–444; May 28, 2015.

About the Author

Yoshua Bengio is a professor of computer science at the University of Montreal and one of the pioneers in developing the deep-learning methods that have sparked the current revival of artificial intelligence.

Section 3: Artificial Intelligence at Work

What "Self-Driving" Cars Will Really Look Like

By Steven E. Shladover

Soon electronic chauffeurs will take us wherever we want to go, whenever we want, in complete safety—as long as we do not need to make any left turns across traffic. Changing road surfaces are a problem, too. So are snow and ice. It will be crucial to avoid traffic cops, crossing guards and emergency vehicles. And in an urban environment where pedestrians are likely to run out in front of the car, we should probably just walk or take the subway.

All these simple, everyday encounters for human drivers pose enormous problems for computers that will take time, money and effort to solve. Yet much of the public is becoming convinced that fully automated vehicles are just around the corner.

What created this disconnect? Part of the problem is terminology. The popular media applies the descriptors "autonomous," "driverless" and "self-driving" indiscriminately to technologies that are very different from one another, blurring important distinctions. And the automotive industry has not helped clarify matters. Marketers working for vehicle manufacturers, equipment suppliers and technology companies carefully compose publicity materials to support a wide range of interpretations about the amount of driving their products automate. Journalists who cover the field have an incentive to adopt the most optimistic forecasts—they are simply more exciting. The result of this feedback loop is a spiral of increasingly unrealistic expectations.

This confusion is unfortunate because automated driving is coming, and it could save lives, reduce pollution and conserve fuel. But it will not happen in quite the way you have been told.

Defining Automated Driving

Driving is a much more complex activity than most people appreciate. It involves a broad range of skills and actions, some of which are easier to automate than others. Maintaining speed on an open road is simple, which is why conventional cruise-control systems have been doing it automatically for decades. As technology has advanced, engineers have been able to automate additional driving subtasks. Widely available adaptive cruise-control systems now maintain proper speed and spacing behind other vehicles. Lane-keeping systems, such as those in new models from Mercedes-Benz and Infiniti, use cameras, sensors and steering control to keep a vehicle centered in its lane. Cars are pretty smart these days. Yet it is an enormous leap from such systems to fully automated driving.

A five-level taxonomy defined by SAE International (formerly the Society of Automotive Engineers) is useful for clarifying our thinking about automated driving. The first three rungs on this ladder of increasing automation (excluding level zero, for no automation) are occupied by technologies that rely on humans for emergency backup. Adaptive cruise control, lane-keeping systems, and the like belong to level one. Level-two systems combine the functions of level-one technologies–the lateral and longitudinal controls of lane-keeping and adaptive cruise-control systems, for example–to automate more complex driving tasks. This is as far as commercially available vehicle automation goes today. Level-three systems would allow drivers to turn on autopilot in specific scenarios, such as freeway traffic jams.

The next two levels are profoundly different in that they operate entirely without human assistance. Level-four (high-automation) systems would handle all driving subtasks, but they would operate only in strictly defined scenarios–in enclosed parking garages, for example, or in dedicated lanes on the freeway. At the top of the ladder is level five–the fully automated car. Presumably, this is what many people have in mind when they hear someone such as Nissan CEO Carlos Ghosn confidently proclaim that automated cars will be on the road by 2020.

The truth is that no one expects level-five automation systems to be on the market by then. In all likelihood, they are a long way off. Level-three systems might be just as remote. But level four?

Look for it within the next decade. To understand this confusing state of affairs, we have to talk about software.

Software Nightmare

Despite the popular perception, human drivers are remarkably capable of avoiding serious crashes. Based on the total U.S. traffic safety statistics for 2011, fatal crashes occurred about once for every 3.3 million hours of driving; crashes that resulted in injury happened approximately once for every 64,000 hours of driving. These numbers set an important safety target for automated driving systems, which should, at minimum, be no less safe than human drivers. Reaching this level of reliability will require vastly more development than automation enthusiasts want to admit.

Think about how often your laptop freezes up. If that software were responsible for driving a car, the "blue screen of death" would become more than a figure of speech. A delayed software response of as little as one tenth of a second is likely to be hazardous in traffic. Software for automated driving must therefore be designed and developed to dramatically different standards from anything currently found in consumer devices.

Achieving these standards will be profoundly difficult and require basic breakthroughs in software engineering and signal processing. Engineers need new methods for designing software that can be proved correct and safe even in complex and rapidly changing conditions. Formal methods for analyzing every possible failure mode for a piece of code before it is written exist–think of them as mathematical proofs for computer programs–but only for very simple applications. Scientists are only beginning to think about how to scale up these kinds of tests to validate the incredibly complex code required to control a fully automated vehicle.

Once that code has been written, software engineers will need new methods for debugging and verifying it. Existing methods are too cumbersome and costly for the job. To put this in perspective, consider that half of the cost of a new commercial or military aircraft goes toward software verification and validation. The software on aircraft is actually much less complex than what will be needed for automated road vehicles. An engineer can design an aircraft autopilot system knowing that it will rarely, if ever, have to deal with more than one or two other aircraft in its vicinity. It does not need to know the velocity and location of those aircraft with incredible precision, because they are far enough apart that they have time to act. Decisions must be made on the order of tens of seconds. An automated road vehicle will have to track dozens of other vehicles and obstacles and make decisions within fractions of a second. The code required will be orders of magnitude more complex than what it takes to fly an airplane.

Once the code is validated, manufacturers will need ways to "prove" the safety of a complete automated driving system to the satisfaction of company risk-management officers, insurance firms, safety advocates, regulators and, of course, potential customers. The kind of formal "acceptance tests" used today are completely impractical for this purpose. Testers would have to put hundreds of millions, if not billions, of miles on a vehicle to ensure that they have subjected it in a statistically significant way to the dangerous scenarios it will encounter when it is regularly used by thousands of customers. People have started to think about solutions to this problem—the German government and industry have launched a multimillion-dollar project with that goal—but those efforts have just begun.

The code that will control the vehicle—the brain, so to speak—is not the only thing that must be subjected to scrutiny. The sensors that provide that brain with the data it will use to make decisions must be subjected to equal scrutiny. Engineers must develop new sensor-signal processing and data-fusion algorithms that can discriminate between benign and hazardous objects in a vehicle's path with nearly zero false negatives (hazardous objects that were not identified) and extremely low false positives (benign objects that were misclassified, leading to inappropriate responses from vehicles, such as swerving or hard braking).

Engineers cannot resort to the kind of brute-force redundancy used in commercial aircraft systems to achieve these goals because an automated car is a consumer product: it must be affordable for the general public. Turning to artificial intelligence is not an obvious solution, either. Some people have suggested that machine-learning systems could enable automated driving systems to study millions of hours of driving data and then learn throughout the course of their life cycle. But machine learning introduces its own problems because it is nondeterministic. Two identical vehicles can roll off the assembly line, but after a year of encountering different traffic situations, their automation systems will behave very differently.

Level-Four Future

I used to tell people that level-five fully automated driving systems would not become feasible until after 2040. Somewhere along the way people started quoting me as saying level five would arrive *in* 2040. Now I say that fully automated vehicles capable of driving in every situation will not be here until 2075. Could it happen sooner than that? Certainly. But not by much.

The prospects for level-three automation are clouded, too, because of the very real problem of recapturing the attention, in an emergency, of a driver who has zoned out while watching the scenery go by or, worse, who has fallen asleep. I have heard representatives from some automakers say that this is such a hard problem that they simply will not attempt level three. Outside of traffic-jam assistants that take over in stop-and-go traffic, where speeds are so low that a worst-case collision would be a fender bender, it is conceivable that level-three automation will never happen.

And yet we will see highly automated cars soon, probably within the coming decade. Nearly every big automaker and many information technology companies are devoting serious resources to level-four automation: fully automated driving, restricted to specific environments, that does not rely on a fallible human for backup.

When you limit the situations in which automated vehicle systems must operate, you greatly increase their feasibility. (Automated people movers have been operating in big airports for years–but they are on totally segregated tracks.)

In all probability, the next 10 years will bring automated valet-parking systems that will allow drivers to drop their cars at the entrance of a suitably equipped garage that excludes pedestrians and nonautomated vehicles. An onboard automation system will communicate with sensors placed throughout the garage to find out which parking spots are available and navigate to them. Because there will be no need to open the doors, parking spaces can be narrower than they are today, so more cars will be able to fit in garages in areas where space is expensive.

In urban pedestrian zones, business parks, university campuses and other places where high-speed vehicles can be excluded, low-speed passenger shuttles will operate without drivers. In such environments, limited-capability sensors should be adequate to detect pedestrians and bicyclists, and if a sensor detects a false positive and brakes unnecessarily, it will not harm anyone (although it will annoy the people in the vehicle). The CityMobil2 project of the European Commission has been demonstrating such technologies for several years, and its final demonstration is scheduled for this summer.

Segregated bus ways and truck-only lanes will soon enable commercial vehicles to operate at higher levels of automation. Physically segregating these vehicles from other users will greatly simplify threat detection and response systems. Eventually driverless trucks and buses will be able to follow a human-driven lead vehicle in fuel-saving platoons. Researchers worldwide, including the California Partners for Advanced Transportation Technology (PATH) program at the University of California, Berkeley, Japan's Energy ITS project, and the KONVOI and SARTRE projects in Europe, have already tested prototype bus- and truck-platoon systems.

Yet the most widespread implementation of level-four automation within the next decade will probably be automated freeway systems for personal passenger vehicles. These systems will permit automobiles to drive themselves under certain conditions on designated sections of freeway. The vehicles will have redundant components and subsystems so that if something goes wrong, they can "limp home" without human guidance. They will probably be restricted to fair weather on stretches of freeway that have been mapped in detail, down to the signage and lane markings. These sections of road might even have "safe harbor" locations where vehicles can go when they have problems. Most major vehicle manufacturers are hard at work developing these systems, and next year Volvo Cars plans to conduct a public field test of such capabilities with 100 prototype vehicles in Gothenburg, Sweden.

These scenarios might not sound as futuristic as having your own personal electronic chauffeur, but they have the benefit of being possible–even inevitable–and soon.

Referenced

Technical Challenges for Fully Automated Driving Systems. Steven Shladover. Presented at the 21st World Congress on Intelligent Transport Systems, Detroit, Mich., September 7–11, 2014.

Towards Road Transport Automation: Opportunities in Public-Private Collaboration. Summary of the Third EU-U.S. Transportation Research Symposium, Washington, D.C., April 14–15, 2015. National Academies of Sciences, Engineering, and Medicine, 2015.

Summary of definitions for SAE International's 2014 report Taxonomy and Definitions for Terms Related to On-Road Motor Vehicle Automated Driving Systems: www.sae.org/misc/pdfs/automated_driving.pdf.

About the Author

Steven E. Shladover is an engineer who has been conducting research on applications of advanced technologies for transportation systems for more than 45 years. He has expertise in transportation systems planning and analysis, vehicle dynamics and control, large-scale systems and economics. Shladover helped found the California PATH Program at the University of California, Berkeley, and has served in a variety of management roles, including program technical director and program manager for Advanced Vehicle Control and Safety Systems. He retired from his position as program manager for mobility at PATH in late 2017.

Can AI Really Solve Facebook's Problems?

By Larry Greenemeier

Congress interrogated Facebook founder and CEO Mark Zuckerberg for two days this week over his company's privacy policies–and its apparent inability to prevent the misuse of its social media platform by some promoting hatred, terrorism or political propaganda. Throughout Zuckerberg's apologies for not doing more to protect users' privacy and curb the spread of false and misleading information on the site, he repeatedly reassured lawmakers artificial intelligence would soon fix many of Facebook's problems. Whether or not he has a strong case depends on how his company specifically plans to use AI–and how quickly the technology matures over the next few years.

Zuckerberg touted several AI successes before two Senate committees: Judiciary and Commerce, Science and Transportation and the House Committee on Energy and Commerce. Facebook AI algorithms already find and delete 99 percent of terrorist propaganda and recruitment efforts posted by Islamic State in Iraq and Syria (ISIS) and al Qaeda-related Facebook accounts, Zuckerberg testified during Tuesday's Senate hearing. But the Counter Extremism Project (CEP), a nonprofit nongovernmental organization that monitors and reports on the terrorist-group activities, disputed Facebook's claim the same day. The CEP issued a statement saying it still finds "examples of extremist content and hate speech on Facebook on a regular basis."

Facebook's founder frequently reminded Congress that he launched the network from his dorm room in 2004, and he acknowledged several times that his approach to monitoring content has long relied on members reporting misuse. That reactive stance has contributed over the years to the company's failure to quickly find and remove discriminatory advertisements, hateful content directed at specific groups, and terrorist messages, he said. Nor was Facebook equipped to handle the deluge of misleading news articles posted by Russian groups seeking to influence the 2016 U.S. presidential election. AI is already helping Facebook address some of those problems, according to Zuckerberg, who said that the company used the technology to find and delete "tens of thousands" of accounts seeking to influence voters prior to political elections in France, Germany and elsewhere within the past year.

Zuckerberg acknowledged that software that can automatically identify verbal assaults is more difficult to write, and still five to 10 years away. The main challenges are defining exactly what qualifies as hate speech, and training AI algorithms to identify it across a number of languages. In response to criticism that Facebook provided a forum for inciting violence against Rohingya Muslims in Myanmar (also called Burma) and was slow to remove such content, Zuckerberg said his company was ill-prepared to prevent its platform from being misused. He told senators that, in addition to developing AI software to automatically identify hate speech in the future, the company is hiring dozens more Burmese-speaking staff to monitor malicious activity directed at the Rohingya. He added that until the software is ready, there's a "higher error rate flagging such content than I'm comfortable with."

Facebook has about 15,000 people working on security and content review and plans to hire another 5,000 by the end of the year. "This is an arms race," Zuckerberg said, noting 2018 is an important year for elections in the U.S. and elsewhere–and that Facebook's adversaries will continue to get better at using the platform to spread misinformation.

"I believe that what [Zuckerberg] says is possible, but since the methods and results have not been published I cannot say for sure whether Facebook can achieve the accuracy required," says Stuart Russell, a computer science and engineering professor at the University of California, Berkeley. "A combination of AI and crowdsourced flagging, with proper inference methods to estimate flagger reliability, should be able to clean up enough garbage that posting garbage becomes a futile activity."

AI's ability to determine whether a Facebook post includes or links to false information requires the software to understand semantics and what different words mean in context, says Dean Pomerleau, an adjunct research scientist at Carnegie Mellon University's Robotics Institute. "You need common sense to understand what people mean, and that is beyond AI's current capabilities," Pomerleau says. A poster's ability to make subtle changes in text, images or video flagged as "objectionable" further complicates AI's capacity to help Facebook. Text alterations, photo cropping and video editing make it difficult for software to do simplistic pattern matching as the content spreads and changes, Pomerleau says. A near-term approach that could work, he adds, would be for Facebook to equip the thousands of people it is hiring to monitor content with artificially intelligent tools that help them find and analyze fake news and other unwanted content.

Facebook's AI development is indeed well underway. The company launched the Facebook AI Research (FAIR) lab in 2013 under the leadership of AI luminary Yann LeCun. LeCun, who switched roles earlier this year to became Facebook's chief AI scientist, focused FAIR's research on developing predictive abilities that would enable the social media site to make educated guesses about what users want in order to better engage with them. That includes more customized news feeds and targeted advertisements as well as improvements in chatbots–artificially intelligent computer programs designed to provide information, enable online purchases and deliver customer service. The same algorithms designed to improve chatbots' ability to recognize different languages and comprehend dialogue will be particularly relevant to Facebook's ability to flag objectionable content worldwide.

A recurring concern in both the Senate and House hearings was whether Facebook can avoid political bias when defining objectionable content. Zuckerberg said Tuesday that the company has a team focused on how to ethically employ AI. Facebook will ultimately have to rely on AI to flag content that might be objectionable or require review, says Florian Schaub, an assistant professor of information at the University of Michigan. "They can't hire enough humans to monitor every post that goes up on Facebook," he says. "The big challenge, and the thing that we as a society should be concerned about, is that Facebook becomes the watcher over our morals. In that case, it's a group of people at Facebook rather than society that decides what's objectionable."

Facebook has been in hot water with regulators over revelations that groups linked to Russian military intelligence services utilized the platform for years, leading up to the 2016 election. Facebook discovered 470 accounts and pages contributing to a disinformation campaign run by Russia's Internet Research Agency (IRA). Over a two-year period the IRA spent about $100,000 on more than 3,000 Facebook ads. The final straw that landed Zuckerberg in front of Senate and House committees, however, was the recent revelation that Cambridge University researcher Aleksandr Kogan turned over data on roughly 87 million Facebook users and their friends without their permission to Cambridge Analytica, a political data firm hired by Pres. Donald Trump's 2016 election campaign.

"It seems Facebook is going through a phase of reckoning and now starting to realize how socially impactful their platform is," Schaub says. "For a long time they felt they were serving a great social function in getting people connected, and now they're realizing there's actually a lot of responsibility that comes with that. That seems to be a little bit of a shift, but at the same time this is not the first time we're hearing Zuckerberg apologize for indiscretions on Facebook."

The real question is more about Facebook's will to change than its ability to develop the AI and other technology needed to better protect member privacy and prevent the spread of violent or misleading content, Pomerleau says. "The basic business model is built on sensational content," he adds. "So it's not clear that getting rid of all inflammatory stuff is in Facebook's best interest."

About the Author

Larry Greenemeier is the associate editor of technology for Scientific American, *covering a variety of tech-related topics, including biotech, computers, military tech, nanotech and robots.*

Faced with a Data Deluge, Astronomers Turn to Automation

By Anil Ananthaswamy

On August 18, 2017, a new age in astronomy dawned, appropriately, with a tweet: "New LIGO. Source with optical counterpart. Blow your sox off!" One astronomer had jumped the gun, tweeting ahead of an official announcement by LIGO (the Laser Interferometer Gravitational-Wave Observatory). The observatory had detected an outburst of gravitational waves, or ripples in spacetime, and an orbiting gamma-ray telescope had simultaneously seen electromagnetic radiation emanating from the same region of space. The observations—which were traced back to a colliding pair of neutron stars 130 million light-years away—marked a pivotal moment for multimessenger astronomy, in which celestial events are studied using a wide range of wildly different telescopes and detectors.

The promise of multimessenger astronomy is immense: by observing not only in light but also in gravitational waves and elusive particles called neutrinos, all at once, researchers can gain unprecedented views of the inner workings of exploding stars, galactic nuclei and other exotic phenomena. But the challenges are great, too: as observatories get bigger and more sensitive and monitor ever larger volumes of space, multimessenger astronomy could drown in a deluge of data, making it harder for telescopes to respond in real time to unfolding astrophysical events. So astronomers are turning to machine learning—the type of technology that led to AlphaGo, the first machine to beat a professional human Go player.

Machine learning could boost multimessenger astronomy by automating crucial early phases of discovery, winnowing potential signals from torrents of noise-filled data so that astronomers can focus on the most tantalizing targets. But this technique promises more. Astrophysicists are also trying it out to weigh galaxy clusters and to create high-resolution simulations needed to study cosmic evolution. And despite concerns about just how machine-learning algorithms work, the stupendous improvements they offer for speed and efficiency are unquestionable.

"This is like a tsunami," says Eliu Huerta, an astrophysicist and artificial intelligence researcher at the National Center for Supercomputing Applications (NCSA) at the University of Illinois at Urbana-Champaign. "People realize that for the big data we have [coming] in the future, we can no longer rely on what we have been doing in the past."

The Gravitational-Wave Hotline

The past, in the case of LIGO and its European counterpart Virgo, does not extend back very far. It was only in February 2016 that those observatories announced the first ever detection of gravitational waves, produced by the merger of two black holes. Now in their third observing run, which began in April, advanced versions of LIGO and Virgo have begun sending out public alerts about new potential gravitational-wave sources as they are detected, all to better support multimessenger observations.

This practice may seem routine, but it belies the enormous effort required for each and every detection. For example, the signals being collected by LIGO must be matched by supercomputers against hundreds of thousands of templates of possible gravitational-wave signatures. Promising signals trigger an internal alert; those that survive additional scrutiny trigger a public alert so that the global astronomy community can look for electromagnetic and neutrino counterparts.

Template matching is so computationally intensive that, for gravitational waves produced by mergers, astronomers use only four attributes of the colliding cosmic objects (the masses of both and the magnitudes of their spins) to make detections in real time. From there, LIGO scientists spend hours, days or even weeks performing more processing offline to further refine the understanding of a signal's sources, a task called parameter estimation.

Seeking ways to make that labyrinthine process faster and more computationally efficient, in work published in 2018, Huerta and his research group at NCSA turned to machine learning. Specifically, Huerta and his then graduate student Daniel George pioneered the use of so-called convolutional neural networks (CNNs), which are a type of deep-learning algorithm, to detect and decipher gravitational-wave signals in real time. Deep-learning algorithms use networks made of layers. Each layer is composed of nodes modeled on the activity of neurons in the human brain. Roughly speaking, training or teaching a deep-learning system involves feeding it data that are already categorized—say, images of galaxies obscured by lots of noise—and getting the network to identify the patterns in the data correctly. The training data set can involve tens of thousands, if not millions, of instances of previously classified data. The network learns by tuning the connections between its neuronlike nodes such that it can eventually make sense of uncategorized data.

After their initial success with CNNs, Huerta and George, along with Huerta's graduate student Hongyu Shen, scaled up this effort, designing deep-learning algorithms that were trained on supercomputers using millions of simulated signatures of gravitational waves mixed in with noise derived from previous observing runs of Advanced LIGO—an upgrade to LIGO completed in 2015. These neural networks learned to find signals embedded in Advanced LIGO noise.

There are crucial differences between this approach and LIGO's standard methods. Most importantly, deep-learning algorithms can do both detection and parameter estimation in real time. Additionally, they can easily handle more parameters on the fly than the four that LIGO currently manages. For instance, Adam Rebei, a high school student in Huerta's group, showed in a recent study that deep learning can identify the complex gravitational-wave signals produced by the merger of black holes in eccentric orbits—something LIGO's traditional algorithms cannot do in real time. "For each black hole merger signal that LIGO has detected that has been reported in publications, we can reconstruct all these parameters in two milliseconds," Huerta says. In contrast, the traditional algorithms can take days to accomplish the same task.

Because of its ability to search over a larger set of parameters, a deep-learning system can potentially spot signatures that LIGO might otherwise miss. And while training requires supercomputers, once trained, the neural network is slim and supple, with an extremely small computational footprint. "You can put it on the phone and process LIGO data in real time," Huerta says.

Artificial Eyes on the Sky

Huerta is now working with Erik Katsavounidis, a member of the LIGO collaboration at the Massachusetts Institute of Technology, to test deep-learning algorithms in the real world. "The goal is to have some of these algorithms deployed throughout the third and fourth observing runs of the LIGO and Virgo detectors," Huerta says. "It'll be a good social experiment to see how we react to, for example, neural nets finding complex signals that are not observed by other algorithms."

If successful, such a deep-learning system will be highly efficient at generating alerts for other telescopes. The most ambitious of these telescopes, still under construction atop Cerro Pachón in Chile, is the Large Synoptic Survey Telescope (LSST). When complete, the 8.4-meter LSST will be able to observe 10 square degrees of the sky at once (equivalent in size to 40 full moons), producing 15 to 20 terabytes of raw data each night–the same amount of data generated by the Sloan Digital Sky Survey over the course of a decade. Within that massive trove, LSST's astronomers will seek out supernovae, colliding stars, and other transient or variable phenomena–sources that momentarily brighten in the electromagnetic spectrum and then fade away over hours, days or weeks. The scientific value of any given transient is typically proportional to how rapidly and thoroughly follow-up observations occur.

"We have to be able to sort through a million to 10 million alerts of places in the sky changing every night and decide in, effectively, real time what is worth using precious resources for follow-up," says Joshua Bloom, an astrophysicist and machine-learning expert at the University of California, Berkeley. "Machine learning will have a massive role in that." Such approaches are already paying dividends for precursors to LSST, including the Zwicky Transient Facility (ZTF), which uses a camera with a field of view of 47 square degrees, installed on a 1.2-meter telescope at the Palomar Observatory in California. In a preprint paper, Dmitry Duev of the California Institute of Technology and his colleagues recently reported that a system called DeepStreaks is already helping astronomers track asteroids and other fast-moving near-Earth objects. "We can improve the efficiency of detecting streaking asteroids by a couple orders of magnitude," the researchers wrote.

Similar techniques can be used to search for other transient sources in ZTF data. "Machine learning is incredibly important for the success of the project," Bloom says. The other important component of multimessenger astronomy is the detection of neutrinos, which are emitted alongside electromagnetic radiation from astrophysical objects such as blazars. (Blazars are quasars–highly luminous objects powered by giant black holes at the centers of distant galaxies–whose jets of high-energy particles and radiation are pointed toward Earth.)

On September 22, 2017, IceCube, a neutrino detector comprising 5,160 sensors embedded within one cubic kilometer of ice below the South Pole, detected neutrinos from a blazar. The sensors look for streaks of light made by particles called muons, which are created when neutrinos hit the ice. But the handful of neutrino-generated muons can be outnumbered by the millions of muons created by cosmic rays encountering Earth's atmosphere. IceCube has to essentially sift through this morass of muon tracks to identify those from neutrinos–a task tailor-made for machine learning.

In a preprint paper last September, Nicholas Choma of New York University and his colleagues reported the development of a special type of deep-learning algorithm called a graph neural network, whose connections and architecture take advantage of the spatial geometry of the sensors in the ice and the fact that only a few sensors see the light from any given muon track. Using simulated data, which had a mix of background noise and signals, the researchers showed that their network detected more than six times as many events as the non-machine-learning approach currently being used by IceCube.

Huerta is impressed by these achievements. "If we are developing or constructing these next-generation instruments to study the universe in high fidelity, we also better design better algorithms to process this data," he says.

Einstein in a Box

As important as these advances are, deep-learning algorithms come with a major concern. They are essentially "black boxes," with the specifics of their operations obscured by the interconnectivity of their layered components and the thousands to millions of tunable parameters required to make them function. In short, even experts looking in from the outside are hard-pressed to understand exactly how any given deep-learning algorithm arrives at a decision. "That's almost antithetical to the way that physicists like to think about the world, which is that there are–and there ought to be–very simple mathematical functions that describe the way that the world works," Bloom says.

To get a handle on interpreting what machine-learning algorithms are doing, Michelle Ntampaka, an astrophysicist and machine-learning researcher at Harvard University and her colleagues developed a CNN to analyze x-ray images of galaxy clusters. They trained and tested the network using 7,896 simulated x-ray images of 329 massive clusters, designed to resemble those generated by the Chandra X-ray Observatory. The CNN became just as good as traditional techniques at inferring the mass of a cluster. But how was that neural net doing its job?

To find out, Ntampaka and her team used a technique pioneered by Google's DeepDream project, which enables humans to visualize what a deep-learning network is seeing. Ntampaka's team found that the CNN had learned to ignore photons coming from the core of the clusters and was paying more attention to photons from their periphery to make its predictions. Astronomers had empirically arrived at this exact solution about a decade earlier. "It's exciting that it learned to excise the cores, because this is evidence that we can now use these neural networks to point back to the underlying physics," Ntampaka says.

For Ntampaka, these results suggest that machine-learning systems are not entirely immune to interpretation. "It's a misunderstanding within the community that they only can be black boxes," she says. "I think interpretability is on the horizon. It's coming. We are starting to be able to do it now." But she also acknowledges that had her team not already known the underlying physics connecting the x-ray emissions from galaxy clusters to their mass, it might not have figured out that the neural network was excising the cores from its analysis.

The question of interpretability has come to the fore in work by astrophysicist Shirley Ho of the Flatiron Institute in New York City and her colleagues. The researchers built a deep-learning algorithm, which they call the Deep Density Displacement Model, or D3M (pronounced "dee cube em"), to efficiently create high-resolution simulations of our universe. When telescopes collect data about the large-scale structure of the universe, those data are compared against our best simulations, which are themselves based on theories such as general relativity and quantum mechanics. The best matches can help cosmologists understand the physics governing the evolution of the universe. High-resolution simulations are extremely expensive, however—they can take millions or tens of millions of hours of computing time to run. So cosmologists often resort to speedier low-resolution simulations, which make simplifying assumptions but are less accurate.

Ho and her colleagues first generated 10,000 pairs of simulations, each pair consisting of a low-resolution, or low-res, simulation of the evolution of a volume of space containing about 32,000 galaxies and a high-resolution, or high-res, simulation of the same volume. They then trained D3M one pair at a time, giving it a low-res simulation—

which takes only milliseconds to generate–as an input and making it output the high-res counterpart. Once D3M had learned to do so, it produced each high-res simulation for any given low-res simulation in about 30 milliseconds. These simulations were as accurate as those created using standard techniques, which require many orders of magnitude more time.

The staggering speedup aside, the neural net seemed to have gained a deeper understanding of the data than expected. The training data set was generated using only one set of values for six cosmological parameters (such as the amount of dark matter thought to exist in the universe). But when D3M was given a low-res simulation of a universe with an amount of dark matter that was significantly different than what physicists think is present in our universe, it correctly produced a high-res simulation with the new dark matter content, despite never being explicitly taught to do so.

Ho and her team are somewhat at a loss to explain exactly why D3M is successful at extrapolating high-res simulations from low-res ones despite the differing amounts of dark matter. Changing the amount of dark matter changes the forces influencing galaxies, and yet the algorithm works. Maybe, Ho says, it figured out the extrapolation for changes in only one parameter and could fail if multiple parameters are changed at once. Her team is currently testing this hypothesis.

The other "real grand possibility," Ho adds, is that D3M has stumbled on a deeper understanding of the laws of physics. "Maybe the universe is really simple, and, like humans, the deep-learning algorithm has figured out the physical rules," she says. "That's like saying D3M has figured out general relativity without being Einstein. That could be one interpretation. I cannot tell you what is correct. At this point, it's nearly philosophical until we have more proof."

Meanwhile the team is working hard to get D3M to fail when extrapolating to different values of the cosmological parameters. "If D3M fails in certain ways in extrapolation, maybe it can give us hints about why it works in the first place," Ho says.

Unfortunately, the use of such advanced techniques in astronomy, astrophysics and cosmology is fomenting a divide. "It's creating a little bit of a have-and-have-nots [situation] in our community," Bloom says. "There are those that are becoming more fluent and capable in the language of moving data and doing inference on data and those that are not."

As the "haves" continue to develop better and better machine-learning systems, there is the tantalizing prospect that, in the future, these algorithms will learn directly from data produced by telescopes and then make inferences, without the need for training using simulated or precategorized data–somewhat like the successor to the human-conquering AlphaGo. While AlphaGo had to be taught using human-generated data, the newer version, AlphaGo Zero, taught itself how to play Go without any data from human games. If astrophysics goes the same route, the black box may become blacker.

About the Author

Anil Ananthaswamy is author of The Edge of Physics, The Man Who Wasn't There *and, most recently,* Through Two Doors at Once: The Elegant Experiment That Captures the Enigma of Our Quantum Reality.

Hunting for New Drugs with AI

By David H. Freedman

There are many reasons that promising drugs wash out during pharmaceutical development, and one of them is cytochrome P450. A set of enzymes mostly produced in the liver, CYP450, as it is commonly called, is involved in breaking down chemicals and preventing them from building up to dangerous levels in the bloodstream. Many experimental drugs, it turns out, inhibit the production of CYP450—a vexing side effect that can render such a drug toxic in humans.

Drug companies have long relied on conventional tools to try to predict whether a drug candidate will inhibit CYP450 in patients, such as by conducting chemical analyses in test tubes, looking at CYP450 interactions with better-understood drugs that have chemical similarities, and running tests on mice. But their predictions are wrong about a third of the time. In those cases, CYP450-related toxicity may come to light only during human trials, resulting in millions of dollars and years of effort going to waste. This costly inaccuracy can, at times, feel like "the bane of our existence," says Saurabh Saha, senior vice president of research and development and translational medicine at Bristol-Myers Squibb.

Inefficiencies such as this one contribute to a larger problem: the $1-trillion global pharmaceutical industry has been in a drug development and productivity slide for at least two decades. Pharmaceutical companies are spending more and more—the 10 largest ones now pay nearly $80 billion a year—to come up with fewer and fewer successful drugs. Ten years ago every dollar invested in research and development saw a return of 10 cents; today it yields less than two cents. In part, that is because the drugs that are easiest to find and that safely and effectively treat common disorders have all been found; what is left is hunting for drugs that address problems with complex and elusive solutions and that would treat disorders affecting only tiny portions of the population—and thus could return far less in revenue.

Because finding new, successful drugs has become so much harder, the average cost of bringing one to market nearly doubled between 2003 and 2013 to $2.6 billion, according to the Tufts Center for the Study of Drug Development. These same challenges have increased the lab-to-market time line to 12 years, with 90 percent of drugs washing out in one of the phases of human trials.

It's no wonder, then, that the industry is enthusiastic about artificial-intelligence tools for drug development. These tools do not work by having expert-developed analytical techniques programmed into them; rather users feed them sample problems (a molecule) and solutions (how the molecule ultimately behaves as a drug) so that the software can develop its own computational approaches for producing those same solutions.

Most AI-based drug-discovery applications take the form of a technique called machine learning, including a subset of the approach called deep learning. Most machine-learning programs can work with small data sets that are organized and labeled, whereas deep-learning programs can work with raw, unstructured data and require much larger volumes. Thus, a machine-learning program might learn to recognize the different features of a cell after being shown tens of thousands of examples of photographs of cells in which the parts are already labeled. A deep-learning version can figure out those parts on its own from unlabeled cell images, but it might need to look at a million of them to do it.

Many scientists in the field think that AI will ultimately improve drug development in several ways: by identifying more promising drug candidates; by raising the "hit rate," or the percentage of candidates that make it through clinical trials and gain regulatory approval; and by speeding up the overall process. A machine-learning program recently deployed by Bristol-Myers Squibb, for instance, was trained to find patterns in data that correlate with CYP450 inhibition. Saha says the program boosted the accuracy of its CYP450 predictions to 95 percent—a sixfold reduction in the failure rate compared with conventional methods. These results help researchers quickly screen out potentially toxic drugs and focus instead on candidates that have a stronger shot at making it all the way through multiple human trials to U.S. Food and Drug Administration approval. "Where AI can make a huge difference is having drugs that fail early on, before we make all that investment in them," says Vipin Gopal, chief data and analytics officer at Eli Lilly.

Resources are now piling into the field. AI-based drug-discovery start-ups raised more than $1 billion in funding in 2018, and as of last September, they were on track to raise $1.5 billion in 2019. Every one of the major pharmaceutical companies has announced a partnership with at least one such firm. Only a few AI-discovered drugs are actually in the human-testing pipeline, however, and none has begun phase 3 human trials, the gold-standard test for experimental drugs. Saha concedes that it will be several years before he can say for sure whether the company's hit rates will go up as a result of the AI prediction rate of CYP450 inhibition. For all the hype in the industry, it is far from certain that early results will translate to more and better drugs.

Sifting through Millions of Molecules

Emerging AI programs are not exactly a revolutionary update in the drug industry, which has for some time been building sophisticated analytical solutions that aid with drug development. The rise of powerful statistical and biophysical modeling programs well over a decade ago as part of the growth of the field of bioinformatics–the quest to use computational tools to derive biological insights from large amounts of data–led to tools that can predict the properties of molecules. But these programs have been limited by scientists' incomplete understanding of how molecules interact: they cannot tell conventional software how to find insights in data when they do not know what elements of the data are most important and how they relate to one another. Imbued with the ability to derive their own insights into which data elements matter, newer AI programs can extract better predictions for a wider range of variables.

AI tools tackle different aspects of drug discovery in several ways. Some AI companies, for example, are focusing on the problem of designing a drug that can safely and effectively work on a known target–usually a specific, well-studied protein that is associated with a disease. The goal is typically to come up with a molecule that can chemically bind to the target protein and modify it so that it no longer contributes to the disease or its symptoms. Cyclica, a Canadian firm, puts its software to work on matching the biophysical structures and biochemical properties of millions of molecules to the structures and properties of some 150,000 proteins to uncover molecules likely to bind to target proteins, as well as those to avoid.

But molecules that are good candidates as drugs still have to jump through other hoops. Those include making it through the gut into the bloodstream without being immediately broken down by the liver or metabolic processes; working in a particular organ such as the kidney without disrupting other organs; avoiding binding to and incapacitating any of the thousands of other proteins in the human body that are important to health; and breaking down and leaving the body before drug levels become potentially dangerous. Cyclica's AI software takes all those requirements into consideration. "A molecule that can interact with a protein target can usually interact with upward of 300 proteins," Cyclica's CEO Naheed Kurji says. "If you're designing a molecule, it behooves you to consider the other 299 interactions that could have disastrous effects in humans."

There is growing recognition among biomedical researchers that complex diseases such as cancer and Alzheimer's involve hundreds of proteins, and hitting just one of them is not likely to be disruptive enough. Cyclica is attempting to find individual compounds that can interact with dozens of target proteins yet avoid interacting with hundreds of other proteins, Kurji explains. Currently under development, he adds, is the incorporation of a wealth of anonymized global genetic data about variations in proteins, so that the software can specify which patients the candidate drugs would work best on.

Kurji claims that together these features will eventually be able to shave five years off the typical seven-year-long time frame for bringing a candidate drug from initial identification to human trials.

Merck and Bayer are among the big pharma companies that have announced partnerships with Cyclica. As is the case with most AI-pharma partnerships, the companies are not releasing much insight into exactly what AI-generated drug candidates may be coming out of the collaborations. But Cyclica has shared some details of its successes in identifying a key target protein linked to already FDA-approved drugs for systemic scleroderma, an autoimmune disease of the skin and other organs, as well as one linked to the Ebola virus. Each drug is already FDA-approved for the treatment of other disorders–HIV and depression, respectively–which means they both could be quickly "repurposed" for the new applications if the research continues to pan out.

Sometimes researchers identify a target protein that might play a critical role in disease but find that–as is true of about 90 percent of the proteins in the human body–not much is known about its structure and properties. With little data to go on, most machine- and deep-learning programs will not be able to figure out how to "drug" the protein–that is, come up with compounds that will bind to it and meet the other criteria for safety and efficacy. A handful of AI companies are focusing on these kinds of "small data" problems, including Exscientia, which uses its software to hunt down molecules that might work with a target protein. It can produce useful insights with as few as 10 pieces of data about a protein, says the company's CEO, Andrew Hopkins, a professor of medicinal informatics at the University of Dundee in Scotland.

Exscientia's algorithms compare the limited information available about a target protein against a database of about a billion protein interactions. This step narrows down the list of possible compounds that might work and specifies what additional data would help further refine the focus. Such data might come from looking at tissue samples to learn more about how the protein behaves in the body, for example. The resulting new data are then fed into the software, which pares the list again and suggests another round of needed data. This process is repeated until the software is ready to generate a manageable list of compounds that are favorable drug candidates for the target.

Hopkins claims that Exscientia's process can cut the time spent in discovery from 4.5 years to as little as one year, reduces discovery costs by 80 percent and results in one-fifth the number of synthesized compounds as is normally needed to produce a single winning drug. Exscientia is partnering with biotech giant Celgene in an effort to find new potential drugs for three targets.

Meanwhile an Exscientia partnership with GlaxoSmithKline has led to what the companies say is a promising molecule targeting a novel pathway to treat chronic obstructive pulmonary disease. But as with any AI company addressing drug development, Exscientia simply has not been in the game long enough to have generated enough new candidates that could have made it through to late-stage trials–a process that typically takes five to eight years. Hopkins claims one of the candidates Exscientia has identified may reach human trials as early as this year. "At the end of the day we'll be judged on the drugs we deliver," he says.

The Need for New Targets

Finding a molecule to hit a new target is not the only major challenge in drug discovery. There is also the need to identify targets in the first place. To spot proteins that might have roles in diseases, biopharma company Berg applies AI to sift through information derived from human tissue samples. This approach aims to solve two problems that hang over most research into drug targets, according to Berg's CEO Niven R. Narain: the efforts tend to be based on a researcher's theory or hunch, which can bias the results and overly restrict the pool of candidates, and they often turn up targets that are correlated to the disease but do not ultimately prove causative, which means drugging them will not help.

Berg's approach involves plugging in every piece of data that can be wrung out of a patient's tissue samples, organ fluids and bloodwork. These extracted data include genomics, proteomics, metabolomics, lipidomics, and more–an unusually broad range to consider in a hunt for targets. Samples are taken from people with and without a particular disease and at different stages of disease progression. Living cells from the samples are exposed in the laboratory to various compounds and conditions, such as low levels of oxygen or high levels of glucose. This method produces data on corresponding changes ranging from a cell's ability to produce energy to the rigidity of its membrane.

All the data are then run through a set of deep-learning programs that search for any differences between nondisease and disease states, with an eye to eventually focusing on proteins whose presence seem to have an impact on the disease. In some cases, those proteins become candidates as targets, at which point Berg's software can start searching for compounds to drug those targets. What is more, because the software can discern when the target seems to cause disease health in only a subset of patients, it can look for distinguishing characteristics of those patients, such as certain genes.That paves the way for a precision-medicine approach, meaning patients can be tested before they take the drug to determine whether it is likely to be effective for them.

The most exciting drug to come out of Berg's work–and perhaps the most exciting to emerge from any drug-discovery-related AI effort to date–is a cancer drug called BPM31510. It recently completed a phase 2 trial for patients with advanced pancreatic cancer, which is extremely aggressive and difficult to treat. Phase 1 trials often do not indicate much about a drug's potential except whether it is dangerously toxic at a given dose, but BPM31510's phase 1 trial against other cancers provided some verification of the ability of Berg's software to predict the roughly 20 percent of patients who were likely to respond to it, as well as those who were more likely to experience adverse reactions.

Additionally, tissue-sample analysis from the trial led Berg's software to predict, counterintuitively, that the drug would work best against more aggressive cancers because it attacks mechanisms that play a larger role in those cancers. Should the drug gain approval, Berg might do a postmarket analysis of perhaps one out of 100 patients taking it, "so that we can keep improving how it's used," Narain says.

Berg is partnering with pharma giant AstraZeneca to seek targets for Parkinson's and other neurological diseases and with Sanofi Pasteur to pursue improved flu vaccines. It is also working with the U.S. Department of Veterans Affairs and the Cleveland Clinic on targets for prostate cancer. The software has already identified mechanisms for diagnostic tests that could differentiate prostate cancer from benignly enlarged prostates, which currently is often difficult to do without surgery.

Getting Beyond the Hype

Big Pharma's interest in injecting these kinds of AI efforts into drug discovery can be gauged by the fact that at least 20 separate partnerships have been reported between the major companies and AI-drug-discovery tech companies. Pfizer, GlaxoSmithKline and Novartis are among the pharma companies said to have also built substantial AI expertise in-house, and it is likely that others are in the process of doing the same.

Although research executives at these companies have expressed enthusiasm for some of the early results, they are quick to admit that AI is no sure thing for the bottom line given how few new AI-aided candidates have made it to the animal-testing stage of drug development, let alone to human trials. The jury is out on whether AI will successfully make drug discovery more efficient, says Sara Kenkare-Mitra, senior vice president of development sciences at Roche subsidiary Genentech, and even if it does, "we can't yet say whether it will be an incremental improvement or an exponential leap." If many of the drugs that result from AI efforts make it well into human testing, this question will still not be answered fully unless the drugs progress all the way through to FDA approval.

Bristol-Myers Squibb's Saha suggests that AI-aided drugs' rate of entry into the market is likely to remain low for some time.

That rate could pick up dramatically, however, if the processes for testing and approval were streamlined to take into account the ability of machine- and deep-learning systems to more accurately predict which drugs are highly likely to be safe and effective and which patients they are best suited for. "When regulatory agencies see the same value we see in AI, the floodgates could open," he says. "In some cases, we might be allowed to pass over animal models and go straight to human testing once we show these drugs can hit their targets with no toxicity." But those changes are probably many years away, he admits. He adds that it is wrong to imply that AI replaces scientists and conventional research—whereas AI supports and amplifies human efforts, it still depends on humans to generate novel biological insights, set research directions and priorities, guide and validate results, and produce needed data.

The breathless hype around AI-based drug discovery might actually be damaging, Berg's Narain says, because overpromising could lead to disappointment and backlash. "These are early days, and we need to be sober about the fact that these are tools that can help—they're not solutions yet," he says. Cyclica's Kurji points the finger at AI companies that make what he says are exaggerated marketing claims, such as having reduced the many years and billions of dollars it takes to develop a drug to a few weeks and a few hundred thousand dollars. "It's simply not true," he says. "And it's irresponsible and destructive to say so."

But if hype hurts, Kurji insists he also knows what will give the AI-drug-discovery industry a big boost: more high-quality information to feed the various programs. "We rely on three things: data, data and more data," he says. That sentiment is echoed by Enoch Huang, vice president of medicinal sciences at Pfizer, who says that having the right algorithm isn't the most important factor.

The need to feed AI software with large volumes of relevant data is actually starting to change science, as researchers run more experiments specifically with the production of AI-relevant data in mind. Genentech's Kenkare-Mitra notes that this has already happened in immunotherapy drug research. "There aren't always enough data from the clinic to use with machine learning," she says. "But we can [often] generate that data in vitro and feed them to the system."

That kind of approach could lead to a virtuous cycle in drug discovery in which AI helps elucidate areas where researchers need to look for targets and drugs. Moreover, the resulting research provides larger, more relevant data sets that allow the software to point to even more fertile research avenues. "It's not so much AI we believe in," Kenkare-Mitra says, "as a human-AI partnership."

About the Author

David H. Freedman is a journalist who has been covering science, business and technology for more than 30 years.

One of the Biggest Problems in Biology Has Finally Been Solved

By Tanya Lewis

There's an age-old adage in biology: structure determines function. In order to understand the function of the myriad proteins that perform vital jobs in a healthy body—or malfunction in a diseased one—scientists have to first determine these proteins' molecular structure. But this is no easy feat: protein molecules consist of long, twisty chains of up to thousands of amino acids, chemical compounds that can interact with one another in many ways to take on an enormous number of possible three-dimensional shapes. Figuring out a single protein's structure, or solving the "protein-folding problem," can take years of finicky experiments.

But earlier this year an artificial intelligence program called AlphaFold, developed by the Google-owned company DeepMind, predicted the 3-D structures of almost every known protein—about 200 million in all. DeepMind CEO Demis Hassabis and senior staff research scientist John Jumper were jointly awarded this year's $3-million Breakthrough Prize in Life Sciences for the achievement, which opens the door for applications that range from expanding our understanding of basic molecular biology to accelerating drug development.

DeepMind developed AlphaFold soon after its AlphaGo AI made headlines in 2016 by beating world Go champion Lee Sedol at the game. But the goal was always to develop AI that could tackle important problems in science, Hassabis says. DeepMind has made the structures of proteins from nearly every species for which amino acid sequences exist freely available in a public database.

Scientific American spoke with Hassabis about developing AlphaFold, some of its most exciting potential applications and the ethical considerations of highly sophisticated AI.

[An edited transcript of the interview follows.]

Q: Why did you decide to create AlphaFold, and how did you get to the point where it can now fold practically every known protein?

A: We pretty much started the project roughly the day after we came back from the AlphaGo match in Seoul, where we beat Lee Sedol, the world [Go] champion. I was talking to Dave Silver, the project lead on AlphaGo, and we were discussing "What's the next big project that DeepMind should do?" I was feeling like it was time to tackle something really hard in science because we had just solved more or less the pinnacle of games AI. I wanted to finally apply the AI to real-world domains. That's always been the mission of DeepMind: to develop general-purpose algorithms that could be applied really generally across many, many problems. We started off with games because it was really efficient to develop things and test things out in games for various reasons. But ultimately, that was never the end goal. The end goal was [to develop] things like AlphaFold.

It's been a mammoth project–about five or six years' worth of work before CASP14 [Critical Assessment of Structure Prediction, a protein-folding competition]. We had an earlier version at the CASP13 competition, and that was AlphaFold 1. That was state of the art, you know, a good deal better than anyone had done before and I think one of the first times that machine learning had been used as the core component of a system to try and crack this problem. That gave us the confidence to push it even further. We had to reengineer things for AlphaFold 2 and put a whole bunch of new ideas in there and also bring onto the team some more specialists–biologists and chemists and biophysicists who worked in protein folding–and combine them with our engineering and machine-learning team.

I've been working on and thinking about general AI for my whole career, even back at university. I tend to note down scientific problems I think one day could be amenable to the types of algorithms we build, and protein folding was right up there for me always, since the 1990s. I've had many, many biologist friends who used to go on about this to me all the time.

Q: Were you surprised that AlphaFold was so successful?

A: Yeah, it was surprising, actually. I think it's definitely been the hardest thing we've done, and I would also say the most complex system we've ever built. The *Nature* paper that describes all the methods, with the supplementary information and technical details, is 60 pages long. There are 32 different component algorithms, and each of them is needed. It's a pretty complicated architecture, and it needed a lot of innovation. That's why it took so long. It was really important to have all these different inputs from different backgrounds and disciplines. And I think something we do uniquely well at DeepMind is mix that together–not just machine learning and engineering.

But there was a difficult period after AlphaFold 1. What we did first was we tried to push AlphaFold 1 to the maximum. And we realized about six months after CASP13 that it was not going to reach the atomic accuracy we wanted to actually solve the problem and be useful to experimentalists and biologists. So I made the decision that we needed to go back to the drawing board and take the knowledge we had acquired, including where it worked and where it didn't work, and then see if we could really go back to almost a brainstorming stage with that experience and that knowledge and come up with a whole bunch of new ideas and new architectures. We did that, and ultimately that worked. But for about six months to a year after that reset, things got worse, not better. The AlphaFold 2 system, the early one, was much worse than AlphaFold 1. It can be very scary during the period where you seem to be going backward in terms of accuracy. Fortunately, that's where our experience in games and all the other AI systems we built before then came into play. I'd seen us go through that valley of death and then get out the other side.

Q: Can you explain, on a very simple level, how AlphaFold works?

A: It's a pretty complicated thing. And we don't know a lot of things for sure. It's clear that AlphaFold 2 is learning something implicit about the structure of chemistry and physics. It sort of knows what things might be plausible. It's learned that through seeing real protein structures, the ones that we know of. But also, one of the innovations we had was to do something called self-distillation, which is: get an early version of AlphaFold 2 to predict lots of structures—but also to predict the confidence level in those predictions.

One of the things we built in was this understanding of chemical bond angles and also evolutionary history using a process called multisequence alignment. These bring in some constraints, which help to narrow the search space of possible protein structures. The search space is too huge to do by brute force. But obviously, real-world physics solves this somehow because proteins fold up in nanoseconds or milliseconds. Effectively, we're trying to reverse engineer that process by learning from the output examples. I think AlphaFold has captured something quite deep about the physics and the chemistry of molecules.

Q: The fascinating thing about AI in general is that it's kind of a black box. But ultimately, it seems like it's learning actual rules about the natural world.

A: Yeah, it's almost learning about it in an intuitive sense. I think we'll have more and more researchers looking at protein areas that AlphaFold is not good at predicting and asking, "Are they actually disordered in biology when the protein doesn't have a clear shape, when it's not interacting with something? About 30 percent of proteins [from organisms with a nucleus] are thought to be disordered. A lot of those kinds of proteins are implicated in disease, such as neurodegeneration, because they might get tangled. And you can see how they might do so because they're just sort of floppy strings rather than forming structures.

The other really important thing we did with AlphaFold 2, which we don't do with machine-learning systems, was output a confidence measure on every single amino acid because we wanted a biologist to be able to really know which parts of the prediction they could rely on without needing to understand anything about the machine learning.

Q: What are some of AlphaFold's most exciting applications?

A: We have a lot of really nice case studies from partners—early adopters—that have had a year to work with AlphaFold. They're doing an incredibly diverse set of things, from addressing antibiotic resistance to tackling plastic pollution by designing plastic-eating enzymes. I've been talking to [CRISPR pioneer] Jennifer Doudna about alfalfa crop sustainability—her team is trying to engineer crops to be a bit more sustainable in the face of climate change.

But there's also lots of really cool fundamental research being done with it. There was a whole special issue in *Science* on the nuclear pore complex. They solved the structure of one of the biggest proteins in the body. And I think three groups solved it at the same time from the cryo-EM [cryogenic electron microscopy] data—but they all needed AlphaFold predictions to augment the cryo-EM lower-resolution data in some places. So a combination of experimental structural data with AlphaFold turns out to be a real boon to structural biologists, which we weren't necessarily predicting.

And then in practical terms, almost every pharma company we've talked to is using AlphaFold. We'll probably never know what the full impacts are because obviously, they keep that proprietary. But I like to think we've helped accelerate real cures to diseases and drug development maybe by a few years.

Q: There's been a lot of hype around AI and everything it can do, especially for science and medicine. But AlphaFold seems to have a clear benefit.

A: I mean, it's for you to decide. But I would say I've had a lot of people tell me that it's the most concrete, useful case of AI doing something in science. I like the fact that we're delivering on the promise of AI. I mean, you could say "hype," but we try and let our work speak for itself.

I remember when we started in 2010, nobody was working on AI. And then now, 12 years later, it seems like everyone and their dog is talking about it. And in most cases, as I'm sure you have to sift through all the time, it's like they don't know what AI even is sometimes or they're misusing the term or it's not really impressive what's going on. But I think AlphaFold is a really good proof of concept or role model of what could happen. And I think we're going to see a lot more of that in the next decade–of AI really helping to genuinely accelerate some scientific breakthroughs–and we hope to be part of a lot more. We think it's just the beginning.

Q: Stepping back a bit, AI has been in the news a lot lately, whether for producing intelligent language or creating digital art. Do you think AI has become more embedded in the public consciousness, and how should we think about its consequences?

A: Yeah, sure. We [at DeepMind] have our own internal versions of large language models and text-to-image systems, and we'll probably be releasing some of them at some point next year. It's really interesting seeing the explosion of developments. AlphaFold, obviously, is huge in the scientific community. But with language and image AIs, it's starting to break through into the mainstream, because obviously everyone knows about language and can appreciate images. You don't have to have any scientific expertise.

But I think we should always be thinking about the ethical issues, and that's one reason we haven't released ours yet. We're trying to be responsible about really checking what these models can do–how they can go off the rails, what happens if they're toxic, all of these things that are currently top of mind. It's our view that some of these systems are not ready to release to the general public, at least not unrestricted. But at some point that's going to happen. We have this phrase at DeepMind of "pioneering responsibly." And for me, that's about applying the scientific method to analyzing these systems and building these systems. I think a lot of times, especially in Silicon Valley, there's this sort of hacker mentality of like "We'll just hack it and put it out there and then see what happens." And I think that's exactly the wrong approach for technologies as impactful and potentially powerful as AI.

I've worked on AI my entire life because I think it's going to be the most beneficial thing ever to humanity, things like curing diseases, helping with climate, all of this stuff. But it's a dual-use technology–it depends on how, as a society, we decide to deploy it–and what we use it for.

About the Author

Tanya Lewis is a senior editor at Scientific American *who covers health and medicine.*

Section 4: Artificial Intelligence at Play

Watson, the Computer *Jeopardy!* Champion, and the Future of Artificial Intelligence

By Gareth Cook

Earlier this month, the nation watched as Watson, a computer system designed by IBM, drubbed the two all time champions of *Jeopardy*. It was a much more difficult challenge than, say, beating a grandmaster at chess. To win, Watson had to navigate the vagaries of human speech, the idioms, the puns, the cultural references - all the things, in short, that make language delightful and deeply machine unfriendly. Journalist Stephen Baker spent a year behind the scenes, as the team of IBM engineers struggled to design and build Watson in time for the show. He tells the story of project Watson, and what it means for the future, in his new book, "Final Jeopardy: Man vs. Machine and the Quest to Know Everything." He and Gareth Cook, the editor of Mind Matters, discussed Watson and artificial intelligence.

COOK: For a long time, artificial intelligence was considered a failure. Does Watson represent a new way of thinking about AI?

BAKER: It's true, the early visions of AI never delivered. It turned out to be a lot harder than many imagined to build systems to handle the complexity and nuance of human communication and thought. You could argue that Watson does not come particularly close, even as it defeats humans in *Jeopardy*. As long as AI continues to fall short in that area–and it will be a long while–many will view AI as an unfulfilled promise.

However, in the last 15 years or so, there has been tremendous progress in functional aspects of AI. They use statistical approaches to simulate certain aspects of human analysis. This would include everything from Deep Blue, IBM's chess computer, to the computers at Netflix, Amazon and Google, which study people's behavioral patterns and automatically calibrate their offerings to them.

What's new about Watson is the extreme pragmatism of the approach. It combines dozens of different approaches to question answering, from statistical to rules-based, and unleashes them on hunts to solve *Jeopardy* clues. There is no right or wrong approach. The machine grades them by their results, and in the process "learns" which algorithms to trust, and when. Amid the quasi-theological battles that rage in AI, Watson is a product of agnostics. That's one new aspect. The other is its comprehension of tricky English. But that, I would say, is the result of steady progress that comes from training machines on massive data sets. The improvement, while impressive, is incremental, not a breakthrough.

Q: Is any of what Watson does based on how the brain works, or is it really just computer scientists trying to solve a problem?

A: The IBM team paid little attention to the human brain while programming Watson. Any parallels to the brain are superficial, and only the result of chance. I would say that Watson is a true product of engineering: People using available technology to create a machine that meets defined specs by a hard deadline. If certain aspects of the brain had helped them design their circuitry or code their software, I'm sure they would have jumped at them. But the feeling was that decoding human thought was a challenge likely to last decades, and they were in a big hurry.

Q: Does Watson reveal anything about our own thinking?

A: I find lots of parallels in Watson to our own thinking. Again, this is not because we share the same design, but instead because we're tackling similar problems. Unlike many computers, for example, Watson is programmed for uncertainty. It's never sure it understands the question, and never has 100 percent confidence in its response. It always doubts. As a machine operating in human language, that's a smart approach.

Q: What sort of tasks is Watson good at?

A: Watson is good at making sense of complex English questions and then digging through millions of electronic documents in search of answers. There's no doubt that we humans understand what we say and write far better than Watson. But it can "read" at great speed. Watson is also very good at a lot of *Jeopardy*-specific tasks, such as "Before and After" clues. If you ask it, for example, about a moonwalking singer who is also a southern city, it will come up in a second or two with: "What is Michael Jackson Mississippi." That skill is not likely to prove too useful outside of the *Jeopardy* studio.

Q: What does IBM hope to use the technology for?

A: IBM has high hopes to sell Watson-based technology, or services built upon on it, in a wide range of industries. Any company that needs to draw evidence or conclusions from voluminous documents, they believe, could benefit from question-answering technology. An early deal has been signed with Nuance Technology and Columbia University Medical Center to adapt the system for question-answering in medicine. Doctors conceivably could ask the machine for diagnoses, or if certain medicines when combined have proven to cause dangerous side-effects. IBM also sees Watson as a paralegal, perhaps hunting down precedents in court cases. I think the most likely first job for Watson will be on technology help desks.

Q: Are there other projects outside of IBM that are similar to Watson?

A: There is a lot of research into question-answering technology. Several years ago, Vulcan Technologies, the incubator run by Microsoft co-founder Paul Allen, launched an AI project, HALO, to teach a computer to pass high school advanced placement tests in chemistry. This project, unlike Watson, was based on knowledge taught to the computer. Since the computer "knew" the relationships between various chemicals, it could reason in a way that would be impossible for Watson. For example, it would assume that water would freeze at 0 degrees centigrade. Watson, by contrast, could easily find this fact, but could draw no conclusions from it. The downside of HALO, as I describe in the book, is that it cost lots of money to teach the machine, and it was anchored to that small base of knowledge and, consequently, inflexible.

Google is also introducing more question-answering into its technology. But the search giant is starting with simple questions calling for factoids, such as, "What is the capital of Mexico?" Google is also doing lots of work on machine language translation, where they use a statistical approach.

Q: What did you find most interesting about seeing Watson being designed?

A: What I found most interesting was how they operate in a laboratory created entirely around statistics. Every clue Watson answers creates an enormous spreadsheet, and each of the variables can be tweaked, tested, refined, and then tested again in a blind batch, to see whether the adjustment affects a broader sampling. I imagine it's a bit like the continuous process improvement made famous by Japanese auto manufacturers. But at least they're building cars. Watson, it could be argued, really produces nothing but statistics. Its *Jeopardy* responses are a byproduct.

Q: As technology like this becomes more common, what will happen to the way that we think?

A: We're already looking more and more to our networks for answers. (Just watch anyone with an iPhone.) This trend is bound to accelerate as more sophisticated technologies, like Watson's, become available. As this happens, I think we'll start to view general knowledge as a lower commodity. To succeed in the knowledge economy, people increasingly will have to put knowledge to work, coming up with original ideas. Those who fail in this are likely to be displaced by machines.

But this isn't just an economic issue. There's also the question of what we need and want in our heads to have happier and more fulfilling lives. After all, a person who outsources knowledge-work to the network might end up struggling to carry on interesting conversations, or to make friends. We shouldn't forget that Watson and its ilk are just powerful tools–and that we're the ones with brains.

About the Author

Gareth Cook is a Pulitzer Prize–winning journalist who edits Scientific American's *Mind Matters online news column.*

How the Computer Beat the Go Player

By Christof Koch

God moves the player,
he in turn, the piece.
But what god beyond
God begins the round
of dust and time and
sleep and agonies?

–Jorge Luis Borges,
from "Chess," 1960

The victory in March of the computer program AlphaGo over one of the world's top handful of go players marks the highest accomplishment to date for the burgeoning field of machine learning and intelligence. The computer beat Lee Se-dol at go, a very old and traditional board game, at a highly publicized tournament in Seoul in a 4–1 rout. With this defeat, computers have bettered people in the last of the classical board games, this one known for its depth and simplicity. An era is over, and a new one has begun. The methods underlying AlphaGo, and its recent victory, have startling implications for the future of machine intelligence.

Coming Out of Nowhere

The ascent of AlphaGo to the top of the go world has been stunning and quite distinct from the trajectory of machines playing chess. Over a period of more than a decade a dedicated team of hardware and software engineers hired by IBM built and programmed a special-purpose supercomputer named Deep Blue that did one thing and one thing only: play chess by evaluating 200 million board positions per second. In a widely expected development, the IBM team challenged then reigning world chess champion Garry Kasparov. In a six-game match played in 1996, Kasparov prevailed against Deep Blue by three wins, two draws and one loss but lost a year later in a historic rematch 3.5 to 2.5. (Scoring rules permit half points in the case of a draw.)

Chess is a classic game of strategy, similar to tic-tac-toe (noughts and crosses), checkers (draughts), Reversi (Othello), backgammon and go, in which players take turns placing or moving pieces. Unlike games where players see only their own cards and all discarded cards, players have full access to relevant information, with chance playing no role.

The rules of go are considerably simpler than those of chess. Black and White sides each have access to a bowl of black and white stones, and each places one in turn on a 19-by-19 grid. Once placed, stones do not move. The intent of the game, originating in China more than 2,500 years ago, is to completely surround opposite stones. Such encircled stones are considered captured and are removed from the board. Out of this sheer simplicity, great beauty arises–complex battles between Black and White armies that span from the corners to the center of the board.

Strictly logical games, such as chess and go, can be characterized by how many possible positions can arise–a measure that defines their complexity. Depending on the phase of the game, players must pick one out of a small number of possible moves. A typical chess game may have 10^{120} possible moves, a huge number, considering there are only about 10^{80} atoms in the entire observable universe of galaxies, stars, planets, dogs, trees, people. But go's complexity is much bigger–at 10^{360} possible moves. This is a number beyond imagination and renders any thought of exhaustively evaluating all possible moves utterly unrealistic.

Given this virtually illimitable complexity, go is, much more than chess, about recognizing patterns that arise when clutches of stones surround empty spaces. Players perceive, consciously or not, relationships among groups of stones and talk about such seemingly fuzzy concepts as "light" and "heavy" shapes of stones and *aji*, meaning latent possibilities. Such concepts, however, are much harder to capture algorithmically than the formal rules of the game. Accordingly, computer go programs struggled compared with their chess counterparts, and none had ever beat a professional human under regular tournament conditions. Such an event was prognosticated to be at least a decade away.

And then AlphaGo burst into public consciousness via an article in one of the world's most respected science magazines, *Nature*, on January 28 of this year. Its software was developed by a 20-person team under erstwhile chess child prodigy and neuroscientist turned AI pioneer Demis Hassabis. (His London-based DeepMind Technologies was acquired in 2014 by Google.) Most intriguingly, the *Nature* article revealed that AlphaGo had played against the winner of the European go championship, Fan Hui, in October 2015 and won 5 to 0 without handicapping the human player, an unheard-of event. What is noteworthy is that AlphaGo's algorithms do not contain any genuinely novel insights or breakthroughs. The software combines good old-fashioned neural network algorithms and machine-learning techniques with superb software engineering running on powerful but fairly standard hardware–48 central processing units (CPUs) augmented by eight graphics processing units (GPUs) developed to render 3-D graphics for the gaming communities and exquisitely powered for running certain mathematical operations.

At the heart of the computations are neural networks, distant descendants of neuronal circuits operating in biological brains. Multiple layers of artificial neurons process the input–the positions of stones on the 19-by-19 go board–and derive increasingly more abstract representations of various aspects of the game using something called convolutional networks. This same technology has made possible recent breakout performances in automatic image recognition–labeling, for example, all images posted to Facebook.

For any particular board position, two neural networks operate in tandem to optimize performance. A "policy network" reduces the breadth of the game by limiting the number of moves for a particular board position. It does so by learning to choose a small range of good moves for that position. A "value network" then estimates how likely a given board position will lead to a win without chasing down every node of the search tree. The policy network generates possible moves that the value network then judges on their likelihood to vanquish the opponent. These are processed using a technique called a Monte Carlo tree search, which can lead to optimal behavior even if only a tiny fraction of the complete game tree is explored.

A Monte Carlo tree search by itself was not good enough for these programs to compete at the world-class level. That required giving AlphaGo the ability to learn, initially by exposing it to previously played games of professional go players and subsequently by enabling the program to play millions of games against itself, continuously improving its performance in the process.

In the first stage, a 13-layer policy neural network started as a blank slate–with no prior exposure to go. It was then trained on 30 million board positions from 160,000 real-life games taken from a go database. That number represents far more games than any professional player would encounter in a lifetime. Each board position was paired with the actual move chosen by the player (which is why this technique is called supervised learning), and the connections among the simulated neurons in the network were adjusted using so-called deep-machine-learning techniques to make the network more likely to pick the better move the next time. The network was then tested by giving it a board position from a game it had previously never seen. It accurately, though far from perfectly, predicted the move that the professional player had picked.

In a second stage, the policy network trained itself using reinforcement learning. This technique is a lasting legacy of behaviorism–a school of thought dominant in psychology and biology in the first half of the 20th century. It professes the idea that organisms–from worms, flies and sea slugs to rats and people–learn by relating a particular action to specific stimuli that preceded it. As they do this over and over again, the organisms build up an association between stimulus and response. This can be done unconsciously using rote learning.

Reinforcement learning was implemented years ago in neural networks to mimic animal behavior and to train robots. DeepMind demonstrated this last year with a vengeance when networks were taught how to play 49 different Atari 2600 video games, including

Video Pinball, Stargunner, Robot Tank, Road Runner, Pong, Space Invaders, Ms. Pac-Man, Alien and Montezuma's Revenge. (It was a sign of things to come: *atari* is a Japanese go term, signifying the imminent capture of one or more stones.)

Each time it played, the DeepMind network "saw" the same video-game screen, including the current score, that any human player would see. The network's output was a command to the joystick to move the cursor on the screen. Following the diktat of the programmer to maximize the game score, the algorithm did so and figured out the rules of the game over thousands and thousands of trials. It learned to move, to hit alien ships and to avoid being destroyed by them. And for some games, it achieved superhuman performance. The same powerful reinforcement-learning algorithm was deployed by AlphaGo, starting from the configuration of the policy networks after the supervised learning step.

In a third and final stage of training, the value network that estimates how likely a given board position will lead to a win is trained using 30 million self-generated positions that the policy network chose. It is this feature of self-play, impossible for humans to replicate (because it would require the player's mind to split itself into two independent "minds") that enables the algorithm to relentlessly improve.

A peculiarity of AlphaGo is that it will pick a strategy that maximizes the probability of winning regardless of by how much. For example, AlphaGo would prefer to win with 90 percent probability by two stones rather than with 85 percent probability by 50 stones. Few players would give up a slightly riskier chance to crush their opponent in favor of eking out a narrow but surer victory.

The end result is a program that performed better than any competitor and beat the go master Fan. Fan, however, is not among the top 300 world players, and among the upper echelons of players, differences in ability are so pronounced that even a lifetime of training would not enable Fan to beat somebody like Lee. Thus, based on the five publicly available games between AlphaGo and Fan, Lee confidently predicted that he would dominate AlphaGo, winning five games to nothing or, perhaps on a bad day, four games to one. What he did not reckon is that the program he was facing in Seoul was a vastly improved version of the one Fan had encountered six months earlier, optimized by relentless self-play.

What's Next?

Deep Blue beating Kasparov represented a triumph of machine brawn over a single human brain. Its success was predicated on very fast processors, built for this purpose. Although its victory over Kasparov was unprecedented, the triumph did not lead to any practical application or to any spin-off. Indeed, IBM retired the machine soon thereafter.

The same situation is not likely to occur for AlphaGo. The program runs on off-the-shelf processors. Giving it access to more computational power (by distributing it over a network of 1,200 CPUs and GPUs) only improved its performance marginally. The feature that makes the difference is AlphaGo's ability to split itself into two, playing against itself and continuously improving its overall performance. At this point it is not clear whether there is any limitation to how much AlphaGo can improve. (If only the same could be said of our old-fashioned brains.) It may be that this constitutes the beating heart of any intelligent system, the holy grail that researchers are pursuing–general artificial intelligence, rivaling human intelligence in its power and flexibility.

Most likely Hassabis's DeepMind team will contemplate designing more powerful programs, such as versions that can teach themselves go from scratch, without having to rely on the corpus of human games as examples, versions that learn chess, programs that simultaneously play checkers, chess and go at the world-class level, or ones that can tackle no-limit Texas hold'em poker or similar games of chance.

In a very commendable move, Hassabis and his colleagues described in exhaustive detail in their *Nature* article the algorithms and parameter settings used to generate AlphaGo. Their explanation of what was accomplished further accelerates the frenetic pace of

AI research in academic and industrial laboratories around the globe. These types of reinforcement algorithms based on trial-and-error learning can be applied to myriad problems with sufficient labeled data, be they financial markets, medical diagnostics, robotics or warfare. A new era has begun with unknown but potentially monumental medium- and long-term consequences for employment patterns, population-wide surveillance, and growing political and economic inequity.

What of the effects of AlphaGo on the ancient game of go itself? Despite doomsayers, the rise of ubiquitous chess programs has revitalized chess, helping to train a generation of ever more powerful players. The same may well happen in the go community. After all, the fact that any car or motorcycle can speed faster than any runner did not eliminate running for fun. More people run marathons than ever.

Indeed, it could be argued that by removing the need to continually prove oneself to be the best, more humans may now enjoy the nature of this supremely aesthetic and intellectual game in its austere splendor for its own sake. In ancient China one of the four arts any cultivated scholar and gentleman was expected to master was the game of go. Just as a meaningful life must be lived and justified for its own intrinsic reasons, so should go be played for its intrinsic value–for the joy it gives.

Referenced

Mastering the Game of Go with Deep Neural Networks and Tree Search. David Silver et al. in *Nature*, Vol. 529, pages 484–489; January 28, 2016.

About the Author

Christof Koch is chief scientist of MindScope at the Allen Institute for Brain Science and of the Tiny Blue Dot Foundation, as well as author of The Feeling of Life Itself–Why Consciousness Is Widespread but Can't Be Computed *(MIT Press, 2019). He is on* Scientific American*'s board of advisers.*

Is Art Created by AI Really Art?

By David Pogue

You've probably heard that automation is becoming commonplace in more fields of human endeavor. Or, in headline-speak: "Are Robots Coming for Your Job?"

You may also have heard that the last bastions of human exclusivity will probably be creativity and artistic judgment. Robots will be washing our windows long before they start creating masterpieces. Right?

Not necessarily. In reporting a story for *CBS Sunday Morning*, for example, I recently visited Rutgers University's Art and Artificial Intelligence Laboratory, where Ahmed Elgammal's team has created artificial-intelligence software that generates beautiful, original paintings.

Software is doing well at composing music, too. At Amper Music (www.ampermusic.com), you can specify what kind of music you want based on mood, instrumentation, tempo and duration. You click "Render," and boom! There's your original piece, not only composed but also "performed" and "mixed" by AI software.

Amper's software doesn't write melodies. It does, however, produce impressive background tracks–that is, mood music. This company is going after stock-music houses, companies that sell ready-to-download music for reality TV shows, Web videos, student movies, and so on.

I found these examples of robotically generated art and music to be polished and appealing. But something kept nagging at me: What happens in a world where effort and scarcity are no longer part of the definition of art?

A mass-produced print of the *Mona Lisa* is worth less than the actual Leonardo painting. Why? Scarcity–there's only one of the original. But Amper churns out another professional-quality original piece of music every time you click "Render." Elgammal's AI painter can spew out another 1,000 original works of art with every tap of the enter key. It puts us in a weird hybrid world where works of art are unique—every painting is different—but require almost zero human effort to produce. Should anyone pay for these things? And if an artist puts AI masterpieces up for sale, what should the price be?

That's not just a thought experiment, either. Soon the question "What's the value of AI artwork and music?" will start impacting flesh-and-blood consumers. It has already, in fact.

Last year the music-streaming service Spotify lured AI researcher François Pachet away from Sony, where he'd been working on AI software that writes music.

Earlier, reporters at the online trade publication Music Business Worldwide discovered something fishy about many of Spotify's playlists: according to the report, songs within them appeared to be credited to nonexistent composers and bands. These playlists have names like Peaceful Piano and Ambient Chill—exactly the kind of atmospheric, melodyless music AI software is good at.

Is Spotify using software to compose music to avoid paying royalties to human musicians? *The New York Times* reported that the tracks with pseudonyms have been played 500 million times, which would ordinarily have cost Spotify $3 million in payments.

But Spotify says Pachet was hired to create tools for human composers. And it has flatly denied that the tracks in question were created by "fake" artists to avoid royalties: while posted under the names of pseudonyms, they were written by actual people receiving actual money for work that they own. (It's still possible Spotify is paying *lower* royalties to these mysterious music producers.) But the broader issue remains. Why *couldn't* Spotify, or any music service, start using AI to generate free music to save itself money? Automation is already on track to displace millions of human taxi drivers, truck drivers and fast-food workers. Why should artists and musicians be exempt from the same economics?

Should there be anything in place—a union, a regulation—to stop that from happening? Or will we always value human-produced art and music more than machine-made stuff? Once we've answered those questions, we can tackle the really big one: When an AI-composed song wins the Grammy, who gets the trophy?

About the Author

David Pogue is the anchor columnist for Yahoo Tech and host of several NOVA *miniseries on PBS.*

An IBM AI Debates Humans—but It's Not Yet the Deep Blue of Oratory

By Bret Stetka

In 2019 Harish Natarajan took part in a debate with a five-and-a-half-foot tall rectangular computer screen in front of a live audience of about 800 people. The computer was Project Debater, an artificial intelligence system designed by IBM. Natarajan is a globally recognized debate champion. And the topic at hand was whether or not preschool should be subsidized.

Based on an audience vote, Project Debater lost the contest. But the "it" present held its own, forming logical opening statements. And in 2018 Project Debater won one debate and almost tied in another. Still, the system is fully capable of sounding awkward during an argument-and-rebuttal with an opponent.

While computers will not be ambling to a political podium any time soon, a study published today in *Nature* suggests that this algorithm is inching closer to engaging in the type of complex human interaction represented by formal argumentation.

The researchers observe that the requirements of a debate are outside the "comfort zone" for AIs, which have triumphed in a range of board and video games—not to mention a famous quiz show. In recent decades, startling advances have been registered in AI. In 1997 IBM's Deep Blue became the first computer to defeat a reigning chess champion, besting titan Garry Kasparov in a six-game match. Fourteen years later IBM's Watson defeated *Jeopardy!* all-stars Brad Rutter and Ken Jennings at their own game.

But a lot of competitive computer intelligence has been tested on tasks or games with a clear winner and loser. And it has been amenable to coding that leads to a defined binary algorithmic path to victory. What has eluded computer scientists is a system that can interact with the nuance that enables complex discourse with human beings. Project Debater is getting close to this goal.

In the new *Nature* paper, IBM researchers–comprising a collaborative team at the company's AI research centers in Haifa, Israel, and Dublin, Ireland–report on their system's progress. Following the 2019 debate, speeches by both Project Debater and three expert human debaters were evaluated on nearly 80 different topics by 15 members of a virtual audience.

In these human-against-machine contests, neither side is allowed access to the Internet. Instead each is given 15 minutes to "collect their thoughts," as Christopher P. Sciacca, manager of communications for IBM Research's global labs, puts it. This means the human debater can take a moment to jot down ideas about a topic at hand, such as subsidized preschool, while Project Debater combs through millions of previously stored newspaper articles and Wikipedia entries, analyzing specific sentences and commonalities and disagreements on particular topics. Following the prep time, both sides alternately deliver four-minute speeches, and then each gives a two-minute closing statement.

Based on audience and reader scoring, Project Debater managed to "win" in 2018 against one of the three experts, and it scored impressively high in making opening statements. But on average, it was still slightly inferior to the humans overall. The hurdle is maintaining a meaningful exchange that can take any number of directions, similar to a real human conversation. Still, the study results move the needle in developing an AI system that can understand and produce meaningful linguistic interaction.

"In recent years there's been a tremendous amount of work in developing algorithms that can understand and generate human language," says Noam Slonim, a distinguished engineer at IBM Research and principal investigator of Project Debater since its inception. "The tasks being pursued span from predicting the sentiment of a single sentence to more complex tasks such as machine translation and dialogue systems." He adds that IBM's results reflect a system that, while still coming in second place to a *Homo sapiens* "rival," can engage with an opponent in a way that, until now, was out of reach with other AI systems. Plenty of such systems can generate what seems to be meaningful language with actual syntax. But a big question for the field is whether or not machines will ever be able to emulate actual human reasoning or become conscious.

"On stage, Project Debater is far from perfect, and its missteps reveal just how difficult–and how definingly human–argumentation and debate are," says computer scientist Chris Reed of the University of Dundee in Scotland, who was not involved with the research but was present in the audience at the 2019 debate. "[Yet] the Project Debater research is a tour de force of innovative engineering.... The scale of the achievement of the IBM team is also clear from the live performance of the system: not only using knowledge extracted from very large data sets but also responding on the fly to human discourse."

Natarajan and other debaters are not yet ready to concede defeat to "machine overlords." But for better or worse–one hopes for the better–machine learning is starting to enter a realm beyond the defined rules of chess and Go.

About the Author(s)

Bret Stetka is a writer based in New York City and editorial director of Medscape Neurology (a subsidiary of WebMD). His work has appeared in Wired, *NPR and the* Atlantic. *He graduated from the University of Virginia School of Medicine in 2005.*

Beethoven's Unfinished 10th Symphony Brought to Life by Artificial Intelligence

By Teresa L. Carey

Nearly 200 years after his death, the German composer's musical scratch was pieced together by machine—with a lot of human help.

Teresa Carey: This is *Scientific American*'s 60-Second Science. I'm Teresa Carey.

Every morning at five o'clock, composer Walter Werzowa would sit down at his computer to anticipate a particular daily e-mail. It came from six time zones away, where a team had been working all night (or day, rather) to draft Beethoven's unfinished 10th Symphony—almost two centuries after his death.

The e-mail contained hundreds of variations, and Werzowa listened to them all.

Werzowa: So by nine, 10 o'clock in the morning, it's like I'm already in heaven.

Carey: Werzowa was listening for the perfect tune—a sound that was unmistakably Beethoven.

But the phrases he was listening to weren't composed by Beethoven. They were created by artificial intelligence—a computer simulation of Beethoven's creative process.

Werzowa: There were hundreds of options, and some are better than others. But then there is that one which grabs you, and that was just a beautiful process.

Carey: Ludwig van Beethoven was one of the most renowned composers in Western music history. When he died in 1827, he left behind musical sketches and notes that hinted at a masterpiece. There was barely enough to make out a phrase, let alone a whole symphony. But that didn't stop people from trying.

In 1988 musicologist Barry Cooper attempted. But he didn't get beyond the first movement. Beethoven's handwritten notes on the second and third movements are meager–not enough to compose a symphony.

Werzowa: A movement of a symphony can have up to 40,000 notes. And some of his themes were three bars, like 20 notes. It's very little information.

Carey: Werzowa and a group of music experts and computer scientists teamed up to use machine learning to create the symphony. Ahmed Elgammal, the director of the Art and Artificial Intelligence Laboratory at Rutgers University, led the AI side of the team.

Elgammal: When you listen to music read by AI to continue a theme of music, usually it's a very short few seconds, and then they start diverging and becoming boring and not interesting. They cannot really take that and compose a full movement of a symphony.

Carey: The team's first task was to teach the AI to think like Beethoven. To do that, they gave it Beethoven's complete works, his sketches and notes. They taught it Beethoven's process–like how he went from those iconic four notes to his entire Fifth Symphony.

Then they taught it to harmonize with a melody, compose a bridge between two sections and assign instrumentation. With all that knowledge, the AI came as close to thinking like Beethoven as possible. But it still wasn't enough.

Elgammal: The way music generation using AI works is very similar to the way, when you write an e-mail, you find that the e-mail thread predicts what's the next word for you or what the rest of the sentence is for you.

Carey: But let the computer predict your words long enough, and eventually, the text will sound like gibberish.

Elgammal: It doesn't really generate something that can continue for a long time and be consistent. So that was the main challenge in dealing with this project: How can you take a motif or a short phrase of music that Beethoven wrote in his sketch and continue it into a segment of music?

Carey: That's where Werzowa's daily e-mails came in. On those early mornings, he was selecting what he thought was Beethoven's best. And, piece by piece, the team built a symphony.

Matthew Guzdial researches creativity and machine learning at the University of Alberta. He didn't work on the Beethoven project, but he says that AI is overhyped.

Guzdial: Modern AI, modern machine learning, is all about just taking small local patterns and replicating them. And it's up to a human to then take what the AI outputs and find the genius. The genius wasn't there. The genius wasn't in the AI. The genius was in the human who was doing the selection.

Carey: Elgammal wants to make the AI tool available to help other artists overcome writer's block or boost their performance. But both Elgammal and Werzowa say that the AI shouldn't replace the role of an artist. Instead it should enhance their work and process.

Werzowa: Like every tool, you can use a knife to kill somebody or to save somebody's life, like with a scalpel in a surgery. So it can go any way. If you look at the kids, like kids are born creative. It's like everything is about being creative, creative and having fun. And somehow we're losing this. I think if we could sit back on a Saturday afternoon in our kitchen, and because maybe we're a little bit scared to make mistakes, ask the AI to help us to write us a sonata, song or whatever in teamwork, life will be so much more beautiful.

Carey: The team released the 10th Symphony over the weekend. When asked who gets credit for writing it–Beethoven, the AI or the team behind it–Werzowa insists it is a collaborative effort. But, suspending disbelief for a moment, it isn't hard to imagine that we're listening to Beethoven once again.

Werzowa: I dare to say that nobody knows Beethoven as well as the AI, did–as well as the algorithm. I think music, when you hear it, when you feel it, when you close your eyes, it does something to your body. Close your eyes, sit back and be open for it, and I would love to hear what you felt after.

Carey: Thanks for listening. For *Scientific American*'s 60-Second Science, I'm Teresa Carey.

[The above text is a transcript of this podcast.]

About the Author(s)

Teresa L. Carey is a freelance science and tech journalist based in Maine and a staff writer at Freethink.

Section 5: Ethical Issues in Artificial Intelligence

Demystifying the Black Box That Is AI

By Ariel Bleicher

When Jason Matheny joined the U.S. Intelligence Advanced Research Projects Activity (IARPA) as a program manager in 2009, he made a habit of chatting to the organization's research analysts. "What do you need?" he would ask, and the answer was always the same: a way to make more accurate predictions. "What if we made you an artificially intelligent computer model that forecasts real-world events such as political instability, weapons tests and disease outbreaks?" Matheny would ask. "Would you use it?"

The analysts' response was enthusiastic, except for one crucial caveat. "It came down to whether they could explain the model to a decision maker–like the secretary of Defense," says Matheny, who is now IARPA's director. What if the artificial intelligence (AI) model told defense analysts that North Korea was getting ready to bomb Alaska? "They don't want to be in the position of thinking the system could be wrong but not being sure why or how," he adds.

Therein lies today's AI conundrum: The most capable technologies–namely, deep neural networks–are notoriously opaque, offering few clues as to how they arrive at their conclusions. But if consumers are to, say, entrust their safety to AI-driven vehicles or their health to AI-assisted medical care, they will want to know how these systems make critical decisions. "[Deep neural nets] can be really good but they can also fail in mysterious ways," says Anders Sandberg, a senior research fellow at the University of Oxford's Future of Humanity Institute. "People are starting to wake up to the realization that you just can't trust this software completely."

A growing number of researchers are taking steps to address this concern as AI begins to transform entire industries, including transportation, medicine, manufacturing and defense. A full-fledged fix is still years away but a number of promising plans are emerging. Some researchers test AI systems like scientists test lab rats, tinkering with the inputs to see how they affect behavior in hopes of illuminating the decision-making process. Others attempt to probe the networks' behavior with additional nets or invent new programming languages to better control how these systems learn. The approaches may vary but their goal is the same: to ensure that our machines do not evolve too far beyond our ability to understand them.

Fine-Tuning

What makes today's deep neural nets at once powerful and capricious is their ability to find patterns in huge amounts of data. Loosely modeled on the human brain, these complex computing systems are the not-so-secret sauce of the current AI boom. They are why digital assistants like Apple's Siri and Amazon's Alexa have gotten very good at recognizing speech, and why Google translations are finally comprehensible. They also enable machines to identify images, predict diseases and beat humans at the television quiz show, *Jeopardy!*, and at go, a game arguably more sophisticated than chess.

Neural nets process information by passing it through a hierarchy of interconnected layers, somewhat akin to the brain's biological circuitry. The first layer of digital "neurons"–called nodes–receives raw inputs (such as pixels in a photograph of a cat), mixes and scores these inputs according to simple mathematical rules, and then passes the outputs to the next layer of nodes. "Deep" nets contain anywhere from three to hundreds of layers, the last of which distills all of this neural activity into a singular prediction: *This is a picture of a cat*, for example.

If that prediction is wrong, a neural net will then tweak the links between nodes, steering the system closer to the right result. Yann LeCun, director of AI research at Facebook, likens this web of numerical connections to a box with millions of knobs. By tuning the knobs to satisfy millions of examples, the neural net creates a structured set of relationships–a model–that can classify new images or perform actions under conditions it has never encountered before.

That process, known as deep learning, allows neural nets to create AI models that are too complicated or too tedious to code by hand. These models can be mind-bogglingly complex, with the largest nearing one trillion parameters (knobs). "What's cool about deep learning is you don't have to tell the system what to look for," says Joel Dudley, director of Biomedical Informatics at Icahn School of Medicine at Mount Sinai in New York City. "It's just, 'Here's a few million pictures of cats. You figure out what a cat looks like.'"

This flexibility allows neural nets to outperform other forms of machine learning–which are limited by their relative simplicity–and sometimes even humans. For instance, an experimental neural net at Mount Sinai called Deep Patient can forecast whether a patient will receive a particular diagnosis within the next year, months before a doctor would make the call. Dudley and his colleagues trained the system by feeding it 12 years' worth of electronic health records, including test results and hospital visits, from 700,000 patients. On its own Deep Patient then discerned hidden harbingers of illness. "We showed it could predict 90 different diseases, ranging from schizophrenia to cancer to diabetes, with very high accuracy–without ever having talked to an expert," Dudley says.

Digital Subconscious

Because neural nets essentially program themselves, however, they often learn enigmatic rules that no human can fully understand. "It's very difficult to find out why [a neural net] made a particular decision," says Alan Winfield, a robot ethicist at the University of the West of England Bristol. When Google's AlphaGo neural net played go champion Lee Sedol last year in Seoul, it made a move that flummoxed everyone watching, even Sedol. "We still can't explain it," Winfield says. Sure, you could, in theory, look under the hood and review every position of every knob–that is, every parameter–in AlphaGo's artificial brain, but even a programmer would not glean much from these numbers because their "meaning" (what drives a neural net to make a decision) is encoded in the billions of diffuse connections between nodes.

Many experts find this opacity worrisome. "It doesn't matter in the game of go, but imagine the autopilot of a driverless car," Winfield says. "If there's a serious accident, it's simply not acceptable to say to an investigator or a judge, 'We just don't understand why the car did that.'" It is not hard to picture other problematic scenarios: An autonomous drone strikes a school; a loan-evaluation program disproportionally denies applications from minorities; a system like Deep Patient makes a specious diagnosis. "Getting a very complex system you don't fully understand to behave itself is a profound problem," Sandberg says.

Unmasking AI

Researchers are investigating a number of options in their search for solutions. One approach–called model induction, or the "observer approach"–treats an AI system like a black box. "You experiment with it and try to infer its behavior," says David Gunning, who manages the Explainable Artificial Intelligence program at the Defense Advanced Research Projects Agency (DARPA). For example, by carving up an image of a cat and feeding a neural net the pieces one at a time, a programmer can get a good idea of which parts–tail, paws, fur patterns or something unexpected–lead the computer to make a correct classification.

Then there's the surgical approach, "which lets us actually look into the brain of the AI system," says Alan Fern, a professor of electrical engineering and computer science at Oregon State University, who is leading one of 12 projects funded under Gunning's program. The trick is getting what he sees to make some kind of sense. "An honest-to-goodness explanation would trace every single firing of every node in the network," creating a long, convoluted audit trail that is "completely uninterpretable to a human," Fern says. To extract a more meaningful–if less exacting–explanation, Fern's team proposes probing a neural net with a second neural net. This "explanation net" would learn which neural activity in the original model is most important in making a particular decision.

The hope is to create a prototypical neural net that will help build transparency into autonomous systems like drones or unmanned vehicles. "I don't think we can ever have perfect confidence in any software," Fern says, "but we can do a lot more to make sure the system is doing the right thing for the right reasons and isn't doing something crazy in the background."

That is also the goal of Bonsai, a start-up developing a new programming language called Inkling to help businesses train their own deep-learning systems to solve organizational problems such as city planning and supply chain logistics. "A lot of our customers have reservations about turning over decisions to a black box," says co-founder and CEO Mark Hammond. Bonsai seeks to open the box by changing the way neural nets learn. Most of us, Hammond points out, do not learn–as today's neural nets do–simply through trial and error. We are also taught–by parents, teachers, coaches and YouTube videos. We learn to play baseball, for instance, not by flailing a bat at fastballs until we hit one but via education: We are shown how to knock Wiffle balls off a tee and then to swing at easy lofts until we're ready for a real pitch. All the while we are picking up the language of the game–language that lets us explain what we are doing and why.

Dudley, too, is experimenting with ways to explain Deep Patient's predictions. He is less concerned about the system's black-box nature, so long as the models it generates can be shown to be safe during clinical trials. (After all, he says, "a huge number of drugs we give are black boxes.") Still, he is curious about Deep Patient's rationale because he thinks it might help doctors better understand and treat disease. Although he cannot know why Deep Patient made a particular diagnosis, he can look for clusters of patients with the same diagnosis and calculate their similarities. This exercise has already turned up some surprising discoveries, including connections between diabetes and Alzheimer's disease that predate Deep Patient. The diabetic drug Metformin, for example, seems to protect certain types of patients against Alzheimer's–a correlation that is not obvious using standard statistics.

Show and Tell

Some experts, however, worry that such piecemeal efforts are not enough to ensure public trust in intelligent systems. In 2016 the European Union adopted new data-protection rules–which come into effect next year–that include a legal right to an explanation of decisions made by algorithms. Meanwhile a working group of the IEEE (Institute for Electrical and Electronics Engineers) is developing industry standards that could help define what "explanation" actually means. "Transparency is not one thing," says Winfield, who is heading the working group. "What an elderly person needs to understand about her care robot is different from what a safety tester needs–or an accident investigator or a lawyer or the general public."

Oxford's Sandberg likes to joke that he knows the secret to why the U.S. became a superpower. "It's because they have 'show-and-tell' in school," he says. The quip may be tongue in cheek, but its moral is sincere: he adds, "Being able to explain things gives you a kind of power."

When AI Misjudgment Is Not an Accident

By Douglas Yeung

The conversation about unconscious bias in artificial intelligence often focuses on algorithms that unintentionally cause disproportionate harm to entire swaths of society—those that wrongly predict black defendants will commit future crimes, for example, or facial-recognition technologies developed mainly by using photos of white men that do a poor job of identifying women and people with darker skin.

But the problem could run much deeper than that. Society should be on guard for another twist: the possibility that nefarious actors could seek to attack artificial intelligence systems by *deliberately* introducing bias into them, smuggled inside the data that helps those systems learn. This could introduce a worrisome new dimension to cyberattacks, disinformation campaigns or the proliferation of fake news.

According to a U.S. government study on big data and privacy, biased algorithms could make it easier to mask discriminatory lending, hiring or other unsavory business practices. Algorithms could be designed to take advantage of seemingly innocuous factors that can be discriminatory. Employing existing techniques, but with biased data or algorithms, could make it easier to hide nefarious intent. Commercial data brokers collect and hold onto all kinds of information, such as online browsing or shopping habits, that could be used in this way.

Biased data could also serve as bait. Corporations could release biased data with the hope competitors would use it to train artificial intelligence algorithms, causing competitors to diminish the quality of their own products and consumer confidence in them.

Algorithmic bias attacks could also be used to more easily advance ideological agendas. If hate groups or political advocacy organizations want to target or exclude people on the basis of race, gender, religion or other characteristics, biased algorithms could give them either the justification or more advanced means to directly do so. Biased data also could come into play in redistricting efforts that entrench racial segregation ("redlining") or restrict voting rights.

Finally, national security threats from foreign actors could use deliberate bias attacks to destabilize societies by undermining government legitimacy or sharpening public polarization. This would fit naturally with tactics that reportedly seek to exploit ideological divides by creating social media posts and buying online ads designed to inflame racial tensions.

Injecting deliberate bias into algorithmic decision-making could be devastatingly simple and effective. This might involve replicating or accelerating pre-existing factors that produce bias. Many algorithms are already fed biased data. Attackers could continue to use such data sets to train algorithms, with foreknowledge of the bias they contained. The plausible deniability this would enable is what makes these attacks so insidious and potentially effective. Attackers would surf the waves of attention trained on bias in the tech industry, exacerbating polarization around issues of diversity and inclusion.

The idea of "poisoning" algorithms by tampering with training data is not wholly novel. Top U.S. intelligence officials have warned that cyber attackers may stealthily access and then alter data to compromise its integrity. Proving malicious intent would be a significant challenge to address and therefore to deter.

But motivation may be beside the point. Any bias is a concern, a structural flaw in the integrity of society's infrastructure. Governments, corporations and individuals are increasingly collecting and using data in diverse ways that may introduce bias.

What this suggests is that bias is a systemic challenge–one requiring holistic solutions. Proposed fixes to unintentional bias in artificial intelligence seek to advance workforce diversity, expand access to diversified training data, and build in algorithmic transparency (the ability to see how algorithms produce results).

There has been some movement to implement these ideas. Academics and industry observers have called for legislative oversight that addresses technological bias. Tech companies have pledged to combat unconscious bias in their products by diversifying their workforces and providing unconscious bias training.

As with technological advances throughout history, we must continue to examine how we implement algorithms in society and what outcomes they produce. Identifying and addressing bias in those who develop algorithms, and the data used to train them, will go a long way to ensuring that artificial intelligence systems benefit us all, not just those who would exploit them.

The views expressed are those of the author(s) and are not necessarily those of Scientific American.

About the Author(s)

Douglas Yeung is a behavioral scientist at the nonprofit, nonpartisan RAND Corporation and on the faculty of the Pardee RAND Graduate School.

Your Boss Wants to Spy on Your Inner Feelings

By John McQuaid

In Liverpool, England, at a February 2020 conference on the rather unglamorous topic of government purchasing, attendees circulated through exhibitor and vendor displays, lingering at some, bypassing others. They were being closely watched. Around the floor, 24 discreetly positioned cameras tracked each person's movements and cataloged subtle contractions in individuals' facial muscles at five to 10 frames per second as they reacted to different displays. The images were fed to a computer network, where artificial-intelligence algorithms assessed each person's gender and age group and analyzed their expressions for signs of "happiness" and "engagement."

About a year after the Liverpool event, Panos Moutafis, CEO of Austin, Tex.–based Zenus, the company behind the technology, was still excited about the results. "I haven't seen lots of commercial systems getting this level of accuracy," he said to me during a video call, showing me a photograph of the crowd, the faces outlined with boxes. Zenus engineers had trained the system to recognize emotions by having it examine a huge data set of facial expressions with labels describing relevant feelings. The company validated the program's performance in various ways, including live tests when people reported how they felt when an image was taken. The system, Moutafis said, "works indoors, it works with masks, with no lighting, it works outdoors when people wear hats and sunglasses."

The Zenus setup is one example of a new technology—called emotion AI or affective computing—that combines cameras and other devices with artificial-intelligence programs to capture facial expressions, body language, vocal intonation, and other cues. The goal is to go beyond facial recognition and identification to reveal something previously invisible to technology: the inner feelings, motivations and attitudes of the people in the images. "Cameras have been dumb," says A.C.L.U. senior policy analyst Jay Stanley, author of the 2019 report *The Dawn of Robot Surveillance*. "Now they're getting smart. They are waking up. They are gaining the ability not just to dumbly record what we do but to make judgments about it."

Emotion AI has become a popular market research tool—at another trade show, Zenus told Hilton Hotels that a puppies-and-ice-cream event the company staged was more engaging than the event's open bar—but its reach extends into areas where the stakes are much higher. Systems that read cues of feeling, character and intent are being used or tested to detect threats at border checkpoints, evaluate job candidates, monitor classrooms for boredom or disruption, and recognize signs of aggressive driving. Major automakers are putting the technology into coming generations of vehicles, and Amazon, Microsoft, Google and other tech companies offer cloud-based emotion-AI services, often bundled with facial recognition. Dozens of start-ups are rolling out applications to help companies make hiring decisions. The practice has become so common in South Korea, for instance, that job coaches often make their clients practice going through AI interviews.

AI systems use various kinds of data to generate insights into emotion and behavior. In addition to facial expressions, vocal intonation, body language and gait, they can analyze the content of spoken or written speech for affect and attitude. Some applications use the data they collect to probe not for emotions but for related insights, such as what kind of personality a person has and whether he or she is paying attention or poses a potential threat.

But critics warn that emotion AI's reach exceeds its grasp in potentially hazardous ways. AI algorithms can be trained on data sets with embedded racial, ethnic and gender biases, which in turn can prejudice their evaluations—against, for example, nonwhite job applicants. "There's this idea that we can off-load some of our cognitive processes on these systems," says Lauren Rhue, an information systems scientist at the University of Maryland, who has studied racial bias in emotion AI. "That we can say, 'Oh, this person has a demeanor that's threatening' based on them. That's where we're getting into a dangerous area."

The underlying science is also in dispute. Many emotion-AI apps trace their origins to research conducted half a century ago by psychologists Paul Ekman and Wallace Friesen, who theorized that a handful of facial expressions correspond to basic emotions (anger, disgust, fear, happiness, sadness and surprise; Ekman later added contempt to the list) and that these expressions form a universally understood emotional language. But these ideas are now hotly debated. Scientists have found evidence of significant cultural and individual variations in facial expressions. Many researchers say algorithms cannot—yet, anyway—consistently read the subtleties of human expressions in different individuals, which may not match up with stereotypical internal feelings. Ekman himself, who worked to develop early forms of emotion-recognition technology, now argues it poses a serious threat to privacy and should be heavily regulated.

Emotion AI is not intrinsically bad. If machines can be trained to reliably interpret emotions and behavior, the potential for robotics, health care, automobiles, and other fields is enormous, experts say. But right now the field is practically a free-for-all, and a largely unproven technology could become ubiquitous before societies have time to consider the potential costs.

In 2018 Mark Gray, then vice president for people and business operations at Airtame, which makes a device for screen-sharing presentations and displays, was looking for ways to improve the company's hiring process. Efficiency was part of it. Airtame is small, with about 100 employees spread among offices in Copenhagen, New York City, Los Angeles and Budapest, but the company can receive hundreds of applications for its jobs in marketing or design. Another factor was the capricious nature of hiring decisions. "A lot of times I feel it's coming from a fake voice in the back of someone's head that 'oh, I like this person personally,' not 'this person would be more competent,'" says Gray, who is now at Proper, a Danish property management tech company. "In the world of recruitment and HR, which is filled with the intangible, I kind of wanted to figure out how can I add a tangible aspect to hiring."

Airtame contracted with Retorio, a Munich-based company that uses AI in video interviews. The process is quick: job candidates record 60-second answers to just two or three questions. An algorithm then analyzes the facial expressions and voice of the interviewees and the text of their responses. It then generates a profile based on five basic personality traits, a common model in psychology shorthanded as OCEAN: openness to experience, conscientiousness, extraversion, agreeableness and neuroticism. Recruiters receive a ranked list of candidates based on how well each profile fits the job.

Such software is starting to change how business decisions are made and how organizations interact with people. It has reshaped the hiring process at Airtame, instantly elevating some candidates over others. Gray says that is because the profiling works. He shared a chart showing that the job performance of several recent hires in sales tracked their personality scores, with employees who had scored higher in conscientiousness, agreeableness and openness doing the best.

Machines that can understand emotions have long been the subject of science fiction. But in computer science and engineering, human affect remained an alien concept for a long time. As recently as the 1990s, "it was a taboo topic, something undesirable," says Rosalind Picard of the Massachusetts Institute of Technology, who coined the term "affective computing" in a 1995 technical report. "People thought I was crazy, nuts, stupid, embarrassing. One respected signal- and speech-processing person came up to me, looked at my feet the whole time, and said, 'You're wasting your time–emotion is just noise.'"

Picard and other researchers began developing tools that could automatically read and respond to biometric information, from facial expressions to blood flow, that indicated emotional states. But the current proliferation of applications dates to the widening deployment starting in the early 2010s of deep learning, a powerful form of machine learning that employs neural networks, which are roughly modeled on biological brains. Deep learning improved the power and accuracy of AI algorithms to automate a few tasks that previously only people could do reliably: driving, facial recognition, and analyzing certain medical scans.

Yet such systems are still far from perfect, and emotion AI tackles a particularly formidable task. Algorithms are supposed to reflect a "ground truth" about the world: they should identify an apple as an apple, not as a peach. The "learning" in machine learning consists of repeatedly comparing raw data–often from images but also from video, audio, and other sources–to training data labeled with the desired feature. This is how the system learns to extract the underlying commonalities, such as the "appleness" from images of apples. Once the training is finished, an algorithm can identify apples in any image.

But when the task is identifying hard-to-define qualities such as personality or emotion, ground truth becomes more elusive. What does "happiness" or "neuroticism" look like? Emotion-AI algorithms cannot directly intuit emotions, personality or intentions. Instead they are trained, through a kind of computational crowdsourcing, to mimic the judgments humans make about other humans. Critics say that process introduces too many subjective variables. "There is a profound slippage between what these things show us and what might be going on in somebody's mind or emotional space," says Kate Crawford of the University of Southern California Annenberg School for Communication and Journalism, who studies the social consequences of artificial intelligence. "That is the profound and dangerous leap that some of these technologies are making."

The process that generates those judgments is complicated, and each stage has potential pitfalls. Deep learning, for example, is notoriously data-hungry. For emotion AI, it requires huge data sets that combine thousands or sometimes billions of human judgments–images of people labeled as "happy" or "smiling" by data workers, for instance. But algorithms can inadvertently "learn" the collective, systematic biases of the people who assembled the data. That bias may come from skewed demographics in training sets, unconscious attitudes of the labelers, or other sources.

Even identifying a smile is far from a straightforward task. A 2020 study by Carsten Schwemmer of the GESIS–Leibniz Institute for the Social Sciences in Cologne, Germany, and his colleagues ran pictures of members of Congress through cloud-based emotion-recognition apps by Amazon, Microsoft and Google. The scientists' own review found 86 percent of men and 91 percent of women were smiling–but the apps were much more likely to find women smiling. Google Cloud Vision, for instance, applied the "smile" label to more than 90 percent of the women but to less than 25 percent of the men. The authors suggested gender bias might be present in the training data. They also wrote that in their own review of the images, ambiguity–ignored by the machines–was common: "Many facial expressions seemed borderline. Was that really a smile? Do smirks count? What if teeth are showing, but they do not seem happy?"

Facial-recognition systems, most also based on deep learning, have been widely criticized for bias. Researchers at the M.I.T. Media Lab, for instance, found these systems were less accurate when matching the identities of nonwhite, nonmale faces. Typically these errors arise from using training data sets that skew white and male. Identifying emotional expressions adds additional layers of complexity: these expressions are dynamic, and faces in posed photos can have subtle differences from those in spontaneous snapshots.

Rhue, the University of Maryland researcher, used a public data set of pictures of professional basketball players to test two emotion-recognition services, one from Microsoft and one from Face++, a facial-recognition company based in China. Both consistently ascribed more negative emotions to Black players than to white players, although each did it differently: Face++ saw Black players as angry twice as often as white players; Microsoft viewed Black players as showing contempt three times as often as white players when the expression was ambiguous. The problem can likely be traced back to bias in the labeled images in training data sets, she says. Microsoft and Face++ did not respond to requests for comment.

Many companies now emphasize that they are aware of and addressing such issues. Retorio's algorithm was trained on a data set, compiled over a period of years using paid volunteers, of short interview videos labeled with personality traits, co-founder Christoph Hohenberger says. The company has taken steps to filter out various demographic and cultural biases that would tend to favor one group over another in the personality assessments, he says. But because there is currently no regulation or oversight of the industry, in most cases we have to take a company's word for it–the robustness and equity of proprietary data sets are hard to verify. HireVue, a company that does video interviews with algorithmic analysis of the text and vocal tone, brought on an outside auditor to check for bias, but that is rare.

"This idea that there exists one standard for humans to be and that everyone can meet it equally" is fundamentally flawed, says Ifeoma Ajunwa, an associate professor at the University of North Carolina School of Law, who studies AI decision-making. The assumption, she says, means that "everyone who doesn't meet that standard is disadvantaged."

In addition to concerns about bias, the idea that outside appearances match a decipherable inner emotion for everyone has also started to generate strong scientific opposition. That is a change from when the concept got its start more than 50 years ago. At that time Ekman and Friesen were conducting fieldwork with the Fore, an Indigenous group in the highlands of southeast Papua New Guinea, to see if they recognized and understood facial expressions the same way as people from radically different backgrounds did–a stevedore from Brooklyn, say, or a nurse in Senegal. Volunteers were shown sets of photos of people making expressions for what the scientists called the six basic emotions. To provide context, a translator provided brief descriptors ("He/she is looking at something which smells bad" for disgust, for instance). The Fore responses were virtually identical to those of people surveyed in countries such as Japan or Brazil or the U.S., so the researchers contended that facial expressions are a universally intelligible emotional language.

The notion of a shared group of expressions that represented basic emotional states quickly became popular in psychology and other fields. Ekman and Friesen developed an atlas of thousands of facial movements to interpret these expressions, called the Facial Action Coding System (FACS). Both the atlas and the theory became cornerstones of emotion AI. The work has been incorporated into many AI applications, such those developed by the company Affectiva, which include in-car systems and market research.

But scientists have argued that there are holes in Ekman's theories. A 2012 study published in the *Proceedings of the National Academy of Sciences USA*, for instance, presented data showing that facial expressions varied considerably by culture. And in 2019 Lisa Feldman Barrett, a psychologist at Northeastern University, along with several colleagues, published a study that examined more than 1,000 scientific papers on facial expressions. The notion that faces revealed outward signs of common emotions had spread to fields ranging from technology to law, they found–but there was little hard evidence that it was true.

The basic emotions are broad stereotypical categories, Barrett says. Moment to moment, facial expressions reflect complicated internal states–a smile might cover up pain, or it might convey sympathy. And today, she contends, it is almost impossible for an AI system to consistently, reliably categorize those internal states if it has been trained on data sets that are essentially collections of labeled stereotypes. "It's measuring something and then inferring what it means psychologically," Barrett says. "But those are two separate things. I can't say this about every company obviously, because I don't know everything that everybody is doing. But the emotion-recognition technology that's been advertised is routinely confounding these two things."

One reason for this problem, Crawford says, is that the world of tech start-ups is not aware of scientific debates in other fields, and those start-ups are attracted to the elegant simplicity of systems such as FACS. "Why has the machine-learning field been drawn to Ekman?" Crawford asks. "It fits nicely with a machine-learning capacity. If you say there is a limited set of expressions and strictly limited numbers of potential emotions, then people will adopt that view primarily because the theory fits what the tools can do."

In addition to Ekman's work and the personality-trait model of OCEAN, emotion-AI companies have adopted other systems. One is a "wheel of emotions" devised by the late psychologist Robert Plutchik, which is used by Adoreboard, a U.K.-based company that analyzes emotion in text. All these approaches offer to translate the complexity of human affect into straightforward formulas. They may suffer from similar flaws, too. One study found that OCEAN produces inconsistent results across different cultures.

Nevertheless, researchers say emotion apps can work–if their limitations are understood. Roboticist Ayanna Howard, dean of the College of Engineering at the Ohio State University, uses a modified version of Microsoft's facial-expression-recognition software in robots to teach social behavior to children with autism. If a robot detects an "angry" expression from its interlocutor, for example, its movements will adapt in ways that calm the situation. The stereotypical facial expressions may not always mean exactly the same thing, Howard says, but they are useful. "Yeah, we're unique–but we're not that different from the person next door," she says. "And so when you're talking about emotion in general, you can get it right maybe not all the time but more than random right."

In general, algorithms that scan and aggregate the reactions of many people–such as those Zenus uses to read crowds–will be more accurate, Barrett says, because "better than random" becomes statistically meaningful with a large group. But assessing individuals is more treacherous because anything short of 100 percent accuracy ends up discriminating against certain people.

Many computer vision specialists are now embracing a more agnostic view of facial expressions. (And more companies have begun stating they do not directly map emotions or internal states.) "As the field has developed, there's increasing understanding that many expressions have nothing to do with emotion," says Jonathan Gratch, a computer science professor at the University of Southern California, who specializes in affective computing. "They're kind of tools we use to influence each other, or they're almost like words in a conversation, and so there's meaning in those words. But it is not direct access to what I'm feeling in the moment."

Yet as attempts to map and monetize emotional expressions, personality traits and behaviors grow, they are expanding the parts of our lives that can fall under surveillance. After 20 years of tech companies mining personal data from online behavior, a new, more intimate domain–faces and bodies and the signals they send–is poised for similar treatment. "If you're a Coca-Cola, and you're driving a campaign, and your principal methodology for messaging is the Internet, you know everything about what audience you reached," says Jay Hutton, CEO of Vancouver-based company VSBLTY, which markets smart cameras and software that scan crowds, analyzing demographics and reactions to products for retailers. "But what if we could take computer vision and turn bricks and mortar into that same level of analytics?"

In December 2020 VSBLTY announced a partnership with Mexican brewer Grupo Modelo to create in-store networks of cameras to capture data in the beverage company's 50,000 Modelorama convenience stores and neighborhood bodegas in Mexico and other Latin American countries by 2027. Demand will exist wherever there are screens and advertising, Hutton says. The technology "will be used in transit hubs, or in an airport, or a stadium," he says. "Advertisers are paying millions of dollars to be a sponsor, and their ads appear on screens throughout the stadium, [and] they are looking for validation of that spin."

This trend raises a basic legal and social question: Do the data from your face and body belong to you? In most places around the world, the answer is no–as long as your personal identity is kept separate from that data. "If you would like to know, and somebody's in public, there seems to be no limit in scanning them for their emotions," says Jennifer Bard, a professor at the University of Cincinnati College of Law, who has studied the issue.

Most emotion-AI companies that capture data in public say the information is anonymized, and thus its collection should not provoke concern. VSBLTY does not store facial images or other data that can be linked to identities, Hutton says. Zenus's Moutafis notes that his company's app does not upload the actual facial images that its cameras capture–only the relevant metadata on mood and position–and that it puts up signs and notices on meeting screens that the monitoring is occurring. "Explicit consent is not needed," he says. "We always tell people deploying it that is a very good practice; when you have a surveillance sensitivity, you have to put up a sign that these areas are being monitored." Typically, Moutafis says, people do not mind and forget about the cameras. But the diversity of applications means there are no common standards. It is also far from clear whether people and politicians will embrace such routine surveillance once it becomes a political and policy issue.

Ekman, who earlier worked with the company Emotient and with Apple on emotion AI, now warns it poses a threat to privacy and says companies should be legally obligated to obtain consent from each person they scan. "Unfortunately, it is a technology that can be used without people's knowledge, and it's being used on them, and it's not being used on them to make them happier," he says. "It's being used on them to get them to buy products they might not otherwise buy. And that's probably the most benign of the nonbenign uses of it."

Emotion AI has entered personal spaces, too, where the potential hoard of behavioral data is even richer. Amazon's Alexa analyzes users' vocal intonation for signs of frustration to improve its algorithms, according to a spokesperson. By 2023 some automakers will be debuting AI-enabled in-cabin systems that will generate huge amounts of data on driver and passenger behavior. Automakers will want those data, also likely anonymized, for purposes such as refining system responses and in-car design and for measuring aggregated behavior such as driver performance. (Tesla already collects data from multiple sources in its vehicles.) Customers would likely have the option of activating various levels of these systems, according to Modar Alaoui, CEO of emotion-AI company Eyeris, so if occupants do not use certain functions, data would not be collected on those. The in-cabin systems designed by Affectiva (recently acquired by Swedish firm Smart Eye) do not record video but would make metadata available, says chief marketing officer Gabi Zijderveld.

Aleix Martinez, a computer vision scientist at Ohio State and Amazon and a co-author with Barrett of the 2019 paper criticizing the face-emotion connection, has a photo he is fond of showing people. It is of a man's face that appears to be twisted in a mixture of anger and fear. Then he shows the full image: it is a soccer player exultant after scoring a goal. Facial expressions, gestures, and other signals are not only a product of the body and brain, he notes, but of context, of what is happening around a person. So far that has proved the biggest challenge for emotion AI: interpreting ambiguous context. "Unless I know what soccer is, I'm never going to be able to understand what happened there," Martinez says. "So that knowledge is fundamental, and we don't have any AI system right now that can do a good job at that at all."

The technology becomes more effective, Martinez says, if the task is narrow, the surroundings are simple, and the biometric information collected is diverse–voice, gestures, pulse, blood flow under the skin, and so on. Coming generations of emotion AI may combine exactly this kind of information. But that, in turn, will only create more powerful and intrusive technologies that societies may not be prepared for.

About the Author

John McQuaid is a journalist and author. He reported this story while a fellow at the Woodrow Wilson International Center for Scholars in Washington, D.C. He is currently a Ph.D. student at the University of Maryland Merrill College of Journalism.

Artificial Intelligence Needs Both Pragmatists and Blue-Sky Visionaries

By Ben Shneiderman

Artificial intelligence thinkers seem to emerge from two communities. One is what I call blue-sky visionaries who speculate about the future possibilities of the technology, invoking utopian fantasies to generate excitement. Blue-sky ideas are compelling but are often clouded over by unrealistic visions and the ethical challenges of what can and should be built.

In contrast, what I call muddy-boots pragmatists are problem- and solution-focused. They want to reduce the harms that widely used AI-infused systems can create. They focus on fixing biased and flawed systems, such as in facial recognition systems that often mistakenly identify people as criminals or violate privacy. The pragmatists want to reduce deadly medical mistakes that AI can make, and steer self-driving cars to be safe-driving cars. Their goal is also to improve AI-based decisions about mortgage loans, college admissions, job hiring and parole granting.

As a computer science professor with a long history of designing innovative applications that have been widely implemented, I believe that the blue-sky visionaries would benefit by taking the thoughtful messages of the muddy-boots realists. Combining the work of both camps is more likely to produce the beneficial outcomes that will lead to successful next-generation technologies.

While the futuristic thinking of the blue-sky speculators sparks our awe and earns much of the funding, muddy-boots thinking reminds us that some AI applications threaten privacy, spread misinformation and are decidedly racist, sexist and otherwise ethically dubious. Machines are undeniably part of our future, but will they serve all future humans equally? I think the caution and practicality of the muddy-boots camp will benefit humanity in the short and long run by ensuring diversity and equality in the development of the algorithms that increasingly run our day-to-day lives. If blue-sky thinkers integrate the concerns of muddy-boots realists into their designs, they can create future technologies that are more likely to advance human values, rights and dignity.

Blue-sky thinking started early in the development of AI. The literature was dominated by authors who pioneered the technology and heralded its inevitable transformation of society. The "fathers" of AI are usually considered to be Marvin Minsky and John McCarthy from MIT and Allen Newell and Herb Simon from Carnegie Mellon University. They gathered at meetings, such as the 1956 Dartmouth Conference, generating enthusiasm exemplified by Simon's 1965 prediction that "machines will be capable, within 20 years, of doing any work a man can do."

There have been many other contributors to AI, including the three Turing Award winners in 2018: Geoffrey Hinton, Yoshua Bengio and Yann LeCun. Their work on deep-learning algorithms was an important contribution, but their continued celebrations of AI's importance and inevitability included Hinton's troubling 2016 quote that "people should stop training radiologists now. It's just completely obvious that within five years deep learning is going to do better than radiologists." A more human-centered view is that deep-learning algorithms will become another tool, like mammograms and blood tests, that empower radiologists and other clinicians to make more accurate diagnoses and offer more appropriate treatment plans.

The theme of robots replacing people, thereby creating widespread unemployment, was legitimized by a 2013 report from Oxford University, which claimed that 47 percent of all jobs could be automated. Futurist Martin Ford's 2015 book *Rise of the Robots* latched on to this idea, painting a troubling picture of low- and high-skilled jobs becoming so completely automated that governments would have to supply a universal basic income because there would be few jobs left. The reality is that well-designed automation increases productivity, which lowers prices, raises demand and brings benefits to many people. These changes trigger a parallel phenomenon of vigorous creation of new jobs, which has helped lead to the current high levels of employment in the U.S. and some other nations.

Yes, there were authors who offered cautionary tales and a different vision, such as MIT professor Joseph Weizenbaum in his 1976 book *Computer Power and Human Reason*, but these were exceptions.

The muddy-boots pragmatists started a new wave of thoughtful AI critiques. They shifted the discussion from blue-sky optimism to clearly identifying the threats to human dignity, fairness and democracy. Op-Ed pieces and a 2016 White House symposium were helpful initiatives, and mathematician Cathy O'Neil's 2016 book *Weapons of Math Destruction* broadened the audience. She focused on how opaque AI algorithms could be harmful when applied at scale to decide on parole, mortgage and job applications. O'Neil's powerful examples promoted human-centered thinking.

Other books, such as Ruha Benjamin's *Race After Technology: Abolitionist Tools for the New Jim Code*, followed on how algorithms needed to be changed to increase economic opportunities and decrease racial bias.

Social psychologist Shoshanna Zuboff's 2019 book *The Age of Surveillance Capitalism* showed the change from Google's early motto of "Don't be evil" to calculated efforts "to obfuscate these processes and their implications." Zuboff's solution was to call for a change in business models, democratic oversight and privacy sanctuaries. Scholar Kate Crawford delivered another devastating muddy-boots analysis in her 2021 book *Atlas of AI*, which focused on the extractive and destructive power of AI on jobs, the environment, human relationships and democracy. She refined her message in a captivating lecture for the National Academy of Engineering, describing constructive actions that AI researchers and implementers could take, while encouraging government regulation and individual efforts to protect privacy.

Muddy-boots activists are gaining recognition for their positive research contributions, which offer clever designs that benefit people. In October 2021, Cynthia Rudin received the $1 million prize for Artificial Intelligence for the Benefit of Humanity from the Association for the Advancement of Artificial Intelligence. Her work on interpretable forms of AI was a response to the bewildering complexity of opaque black box algorithms, which made it hard for people to understand why they were rejected for paroles, mortgages or jobs.

Many of the muddy-boots thinkers are women, but men have also spoken up about the need for humane oversight. Technology pioneer Jaron Lanier also raises concerns in his *Ten Arguments for Deleting Your Social Media Accounts Right Now*, which identifies the harms from social media and suggests users take more control over their use of it. Legal scholar Frank Pasquale's *New Laws of Robotics* explains why AI developers should value human expertise, avoid technological arms races and take responsibility for the technologies they create. However, ensuring human control by way of human-centered designs will take substantial changes in national policies, business practices, research agendas and educational curricula.

The diverse workers of this camp–including women, nonbinary people, people with disabilities and people of color–have important messages to ensure that the blue-sky dreams can be channeled into realizable products and services that benefit people and preserve the environment.

This is an opinion and analysis article, and the views expressed by the author or authors are not necessarily those of *Scientific American*.

About the Author

Ben Shneiderman is an emeritus professor of computer science at the University of Maryland, a member of the National Academy of Engineering and author of the recently published book Human-Centered AI *(Oxford University Press).*

GLOSSARY

algorithm A step-by-step process, especially in computation.

algorithmic bias When an algorithm's working is biased toward or against a particular category, either within the program or for external social groups.

approximate To estimate or come close to a measure within a margin of error.

artificial neural network Computer system modeled after the interactions between neurons.

auditory Relating to sound.

black box System whose workings cannot be determined beyond its input and output.

commercialization Introducing something into the market for the purpose of selling it.

enzyme A material that catalyzes a physical process in a living organism.

feedback When the output of a system is used as input into the system again; applies in computer science and other scientific disciplines.

implication Inference that can be drawn despite explicit evidence.

longitudinal Pertaining to east-west coordinates.

machine learning The practice of undirected learning by computers by performing statistical analysis on large datasets.

metadata Data on the organization of other data.

neutrino A subatomic article that is frequently measured in astronomical observations.

oratory The skills used in public speaking, persuasion, and debate.

overfitting Machine learning term for when a program lacks the flexibility to accommodate new data.

parameter Internal metric created by a machine learning system, which is used and calibrated to perfect its behavior.

phoneme Linguistic term for basic sound unit in a language.

policy Behavior defined by an artificial intelligence system.

render To create a visualization for a computer program.

royalties Fees due to someone for the sale of a creative work.

simulation An imitation of something, in AI by use of a computer model.

stimulus Something that causes a response, typically in a biological organism or AI.

theological Pertaining to religious debate.

FURTHER INFORMATION

"ChatGPT: Optimizing Language Models for Dialogue." OpenAI. https://openai.com/blog/chatgpt/.

"Machine Learning: The Power and Promise of Computers that Learn by Example." The Royal Society. https://royalsociety.org/~/media/policy/projects/machine-learning/publications/machine-learning-report.pdf.

Bruce, Peter. "A Deep Dive into Deep Learning." *Scientific American*, April 10, 2019, https://blogs.scientificamerican.com/observations/a-deep-dive-into-deep-learning/.

Courtland, Rachel. "Bias Detectives." *Scientific American*, July 13, 2021, https://www.scientificamerican.com/article/bias-detectives/.

Greenemeier, Larry. "How NASA's Search for ET Relies on Advanced AI." *Scientific American*, December 28, 2017, https://www.scientificamerican.com/article/how-nasas-search-for-et-relies-on-advanced-ai/.

Kumar, Shailendra. "Gender and Feminist Considerations in Artificial Intelligence from a Developing-World Perspective, with India as a Case Study." *Nature*, January 26, 2022, https://www.nature.com/articles/s41599-022-01043-5.

Minsky, Marvin L. "Artificial Intelligence." *Scientific American*, September 1, 1966, https://www.scientificamerican.com/article/artificial-intelligence-1966-09/.

Smith, Dana G. "No Bones About It: People Recognize Objects by Visualizing Their 'Skeletons'." *Scientific American*, September 11, 2019, https://www.scientificamerican.com/article/no-bones-about-it-people-recognize-objects-by-visualizing-their-skeletons/.

CITATIONS

1.1 The Origin of Computing by Martin Campbell-Kelly (September 1, 2009); 1.2 Cybernetics by Norbert Wiener (November 1, 1948); 1.3 Collective Computation in Neuronlike Circuits by David W. Tank and John J. Hopfield (December 1, 1987); 2.1 How to Teach Computers to Learn on Their Own by Yaser S. Abu-Mostafa (July 1, 2012); 2.2 Springtime for AI: The Rise of Deep Learning by Yoshua Bengio (June 1, 2016); 3.1 What "Self-Driving" Cars Will Really Look Like by Steven E. Shladover (June 1, 2016); 3.2 Can AI Really Solve Facebook's Problems? by Larry Greenemeier (April 13, 2018); 3.3 Faced With a Data Deluge, Astronomers Turn to Automation by Anil Ananthaswamy (August 21, 2019); 3.4 Hunting for New Drugs With AI by David H. Freedman (February 1, 2020); 3.5 One of the Biggest Problems in Biology Has Finally Been Solved by Tanya Lewis (October 31, 2022); 4.1 Watson, the Computer *Jeopardy!* Champion, and the Future of Artificial Intelligence by Gareth Cook (March 1, 2011); 4.2 How the Computer Beat the Go Player by Christof Koch (July 1, 2016); 4.3 Is Art Created by AI Really Art? by David Pogue (February 1, 2018); 4.4 An IBM AI Debates Humans–But It's Not Yet the Deep Blue of Oratory by Bret Stetka (March 17, 2021); 4.5 Beethoven's Unfinished 10th Symphony Brought to Life by Artificial Intelligence by Theresa L. Carey (October 15, 2021); 5.1 Demystifying the Black Box That Is AI by Ariel Bleicher (August 9, 2017); 5.2 When AI Misjudgment Is Not an Accident by Douglas Yeung (October 19, 2018); 5.3 Your Boss Wants to Spy on Your Inner Feelings by John McQuaid (December 1, 2021); 5.4 Artificial Intelligence Needs Both Pragmatists and Blue-Sky Visionaries by Ben Shneiderman (September 20, 2022).

Each author biography was accurate at the time the article was originally published.

INDEX